Thirty and single? Well, getcha ass to the Gathering! Wait… what?

Rebecca Twynham hates nature, loves a juicy steak, is not Marked, and thinks wolves come in one form: on four feet and with fur. So when she's hauled to the annual werewolf Gathering by this scary as hell magical vortex, she's pretty surprised to find out werewolves are real. With that new knowledge, she finds she still hates nature, she'd love a juicy steak, and maybe—she might be—Marked. Well, she doesn't see a Mark, but she also has heavy scarring from a childhood accident—or was it intentional? Plus, she really wants to climb the gorgeous Alpha Pair, Aidan and Carson, like a tree. Luckily the two hot werewolves wanna sink their roots into her flower and… The nature analogies have gone too far.

Aidan and Carson have been a strong Alpha Pair for fourteen years. They're tied together by their bond, and ache to claim a woman as their own. But while Carson has always been the GQ ladies' man, Aidan has been the afterthought—the heavily scarred and frightening werewolf who's caused more than one woman to faint.

When they find Rebecca hiding in the Bad Doggie ballroom, they rejoice that they've finally found the one for them. Except with curvaceous, delicious Rebecca, their roles are reversed. Instead of rushing into the arms of sleek and sexy Carson, Rebecca clings to Aidan. Carson should rejoice in her acceptance of Aidan, but jealousy rears its ugly head, destroying their triad before it has a moment to form.

Then things go from jealousy-driven bad to worse when the five families decide there won't be any more Wickhams joining the wolfy family trees.

Oh, right, she forgot that part. Apparently her Wickham cousins are kind of a big deal in werewolf land. Big.

CHAPTER ONE

Blog post by Ruling Alpha Mate Scarlet Wickham on July 21, 8:01 a.m....

Welcome to the Gathering!

Welcome, welcome! The Ruling Alphas and the awesomeness that is the Ruling Alpha Mate are thrilled you could be here!

This is the first year Warden Pairs will be attending the Gathering in search of their mates, and it is a momentous occasion. Please keep in mind that with the addition of Warden Pairs, the Gathering will also host women who are Warden Born. Not all ladies are hunting a hot hunk of demanding love, guys, so keep the drool in your mouths. Also, not all females are comfortable in their fur-attracting skin quite yet. Take it easy on them.

Another thing to keep in mind is that all laws in place which protect the Alpha Marked also apply to Warden Born. In the event you are not aware of the intricacies of those laws, Gabriella Wickham is more than willing to explain them to you in detail. Her very scary mates are on hand to assist you.*

Have a wonderful weekend and may you all find your mates!
Scarlet Wickham
Ruling Alpha Mate and H.B.I.C.**

*Disclaimer: Activities associated with the Gathering can at times involve substantial risk of injury, property damage, and other dangers. Dangers particular to such activities include, but are not limited to: hypothermia, drowning, broken bones, strains, sprains, bruises, concussion, heart attack, heat exhaustion, cuts, abrasions, burns, electrical shock, poisoning, and blunt trauma. By participating in and attending the Gathering, you agree not to hold the Gathering organizers or other attendants liable for such damage including, but not limited to, the above. You break it, but we still ain't buying it.

**H.B.I.C.: Head Bitch In Charge

~~≈~~

Blog post by Ruling Alpha Mate Scarlet Wickham on July 21, 8:10 a.m.…

Welcome to the Gathering Part Two

It has been brought to my attention that not all women summoned to the Gathering have experienced orientation prior to said summoning. In the event you encounter a distressed female, please direct her to the Grand Ballroom on the third floor.* Gathering organizers (and therapists) are on hand to assist the attendees during this transitional time.

Have a wonderful weekend and may you all find your mates!
Scarlet Wickham
Ruling Alpha Mate and H.B.I.C.**

*Disclaimer: Activities associated with the Gathering can at times involve… blah, blah, blah, see all that crap in the last post.

**H.B.I.C.: Head Bitch In Charge

Mass text message by Ruling Alpha Mate Scarlet Wickham on July 21, 8:23 a.m....

There are bitches with guns. Some of them may or may not look like me. Cover your balls and hide. And text me back. They. Are. Crazy. Also, new disclaimer includes bullet wounds and human-wolf rabies. Peace out.

~~≈~~

Mass text message by Ruling Alpha Mate Scarlet Wickham on July 21, 8:37 a.m....

Maybe you didn't get it. Totally cray cray and they may or MAY NOT look like me. Get them. Bring them. Do not pass go, and no sniffing butts! Penises should not touch orifices prior to orientation, furballs! Also, new *new* disclaimer includes idiots getting kicked in the balls because they don't understand simple directions. I'm out.

CHAPTER TWO

Dirt was the most horrible thing ever created. It smelled and got everywhere and itched when it dried—which meant Rebecca had been wet at some point—and was all around gross. She wanted a shower and a bed. Now. She glanced at the man stomping along the trail beside her, at his wide smile and the way *he* hadn't tripped over every tree root known to man.

The bed would be empty. Very empty. The vast emptiness of the empty couldn't even be put into words it'd be so empty.

The guy grinned at her, his brown hair flopping over his eyes. Had she thought that was adorable?

"Isn't this *awesome*?" Tony? Timmy? Joseph! Hah! It didn't sound anything like those "T" names, but she finally got it right. So, *Joseph* spoke.

"Oh, awesome." She plastered a totally fake, painstakingly practiced smile on her lips. It wasn't a happy one. No, it was the one that said "are you fucking kidding me?" It was kinda toothy and big and her eyes were open wide.

Joseph, the lovely Joseph, who apparently could only read books and not people, seemed to perk up. "I know, right? And around the bend we'll see…"

He was talking nature again. Which, to be fair, they were surrounded by the wondrous world of Faunsdale Nature Preserve, so it made sense.

Why, oh why, had she agreed a hike through the preserve was a good idea? When she'd said yes, she'd managed to sound excited over the phone. And maybe she had been. A little anyway. After all, it'd been a while since she'd jumped into the dating pool. It was as if she played the hokey pokey with her love life. She'd put her left foot in, get it bitten by a blood-sucking evil snake, then pull it out and shake it the fuck about.

Snakes. She bet there were snakes in the woods. Evil blood-sucking ones who walked on two legs.

Joseph pulled ahead of her—his longer legs meant bigger strides—and she stared at his back. Was he one of those kinds of men?

It didn't matter one way or the other. After all this back to nature stuff, she was all about *not* having a second date with him. If this was first-date material, she'd crumble into a fluffy heap of "kill me now" on the next one.

"Coming?" he yelled back to her.

Not likely.

Rebecca cleared her throat. "Yeah, right behind you!"

Like fifteen feet. Okay, thirty.

Then that expanded further and… Was he getting taller?

A large brown and green sign announced they were climbing Fwansis Hill.

All right, she'd reached planet Kill Me Now.

"Joseph?" He did not turn around. "Joseph?" She raised her voice and he turned toward her, massive smile in place.

"What's up?"

Rebecca waved at the sign. "I thought this trail was a three on the difficulty scale?" She tried to keep the accusation out of her voice. She didn't want to piss him off, he was her ride home, after all. "This sign says the hill and beyond is six plus."

"Oh," he shrugged. "You were doing so awesome. I thought we'd go a little farther. There's this great clearing on the other side. We can eat our lunch there."

Now he bounced on his toes like a kid waiting to open Christmas presents. Exhausted as all get out, she moved to follow him.

Doing awesome? Hardly. When he'd told her of his plans, she figured she'd be fine. Hiking was probably harder than walking on a treadmill, but she also did Water Zumba when she wasn't working on her slowly ambling cardio. The hike should have been cake.

Mmm… cake.

She *so* deserved cake after this.

Hefting her backpack higher on her shoulder, she trudged after the man. She forced one foot in front of the other, ignoring the dampness of her socks. Stupid rain with its stupid wetness.

Joseph reached the peak before her and disappeared over the other side. No matter, it wasn't like she'd get lost. The trail was so worn it made her path clear. Plus, some parts were paved and benches were placed sporadically along the route.

For people like her.

She passed one such bench and eyed it longingly. What she wouldn't give…

"Rebecca?" Joseph's voice reached her, and she sighed.

"Coming. Gimme—" *A million years.* "—a minute!"

"I'll get our lunch set out!"

Or he could come back down the damned hill, pick up her fluffy ass, and *carry her to their picnic spot.*

Ahem.

Instead of pouring out her frustrated, borderline rage-y heart, she imbued her tone with sugary sweetness. She'd already established he didn't get the finer nuances of the Rebecca language. "Sounds awesome!"

No other shouts came over the hill and Rebecca sighed. This was definitely the first date and last. If a hike through the forest was this guy's idea of a good time, it so wasn't going to work.

Rebecca slogged over the rise, tempted to let her backpack fall from her shoulders and drag on the ground, but she kept it in place. She imagined she already looked a ragged mess, no sense in adding to the disgusting picture she painted.

She spied Joseph off to her right, standing near the tree line, and it was the first time she realized the forest didn't surround her any longer. No, the dense trees were on her right, but the left was open and cleared, giving her a perfect view of the preserve. Not all of it, but at least they got a good look at the valley below. The area was filled with flowers and a brook cut a path along the edge. It was a gorgeous sight.

Especially the water. Could she rinse off? Or rather, dump her whole hot and sweaty ass in?

"I decided to wait since it's kinda hidden. Didn't want you to get lost. This way, it's close."

Close? Close she could do. And at least kinda hidden meant passing hikers wouldn't see her collapse and mistake her sudden flop as a reason to call forest rescue. She was exhausted, not broken. Plus, no matter how hot the rescue guys probably were, it would be insanely expensive to have them come get her. Her insurance sucked.

"Lead on." She waved her hand and he... smiled.

Did the man never *stop*?

It turned out his "close" was about a hundred yards while hers was fifty feet.

But they got there and the first thing she did when she spied the picnic blanket was collapse on the thing. The red and white checkered cloth bunched beneath her. Yeah, she probably shouldn't lie down because she was so dirty, but whatever.

Joseph-the-Ever-Happy plopped beside her, and she noted the man didn't even have a hint of sweat on his brow. He was going down. Deader than a doornail. He was all healthy and in shape. She'd first poison him by introducing chocolate cake to his diet.

And then bacon. No one could resist bacon. It was like the Borg from *Star Trek*. Any second now biomechanical humanoids would come marching out of the forest. *"Resistance is futile. You will eat fattening chocolate."*

"Rebecca?"

She groaned and raised her head. "Sorry. Needed a second." She pushed herself up and swung her backpack from her shoulder. It took no time to settle on the blanket like a normal person, and then the picnic got underway.

Joseph chatted about… something nature-y while Rebecca became slowly aware of a common theme for their lunch.

"Um, Joseph?"

"Yup." He dug into his pack again, tugging out yet another container. The man's bag was bottomless like Mary Poppins's. Except Mary Poppins didn't bring a vegetarian lunch. Like Joseph had.

Vegetarian. Not a sandwich or hint of lunch meat in sight.

"It looks like you went to a lot of trouble," she gulped when a container of celery appeared. "You could have slapped together some ham sandwiches."

He froze and swung his wide-eyed gaze to her. "Meat?" He gasped. "*Never.* I'm vegan, I thought you knew that. Catherine introduced us, and she's…"

Rebecca's coworker and a total plant eater. Nice.

Rebecca shook her head and slapped on another of those smiles. "Sorry, you're right. I completely spaced."

She was so going to the burger joint down the street from her house when this date was over.

Her comment earned her what? Another smile.

Joseph reached the bottom of his bag—at least she hoped it was the bottom since she'd cry if she saw yet another veggie—and came out with… a white envelope?

She prayed he wasn't one of those weirdoes who was all super appreciative for a date and handed out thank-you cards. How weird would that be?

She swallowed her moan. Barely.

"What's this?" he murmured and extended it toward her. "It's addressed to you."

Of course it was. *Because you're a weirdo card giver!*

With a chuckle, she slid it from his hand and then really did release her moan. The lettering was familiar, the calligraphy easily recognizable.

Rebecca Digory Twynham.

Like all the others, there was no street or return address. It was as if someone simply plopped it in her way.

And now it had been dumped in Joseph's bag.

She sighed. She was totally going to the police station when this date was over. But not before the fast food joint. A girl could not subsist on celery alone.

"Rebecca?"

Rebecca blinked and suddenly remembered she wasn't alone. "Sorry, what?"

He raised his eyebrows and gestured at the envelope. "What's up with that? How'd it get in my bag? Are you going to open it?"

"No idea, no idea, and no." Because she already knew what it said.

The Ruling Alphas of the North American Packs cordially demand…

He frowned and opened his mouth, but she cut him off.

"Look, there's some weird… person…"—she waved the envelope—"leaving these around. I have no idea who it is or anything. It's just…" She sighed. "I'm going to the police station as soon as we finish our date."

"How many have you gotten? Are you sure it's the same person? Maybe it's a mistake."

Ah, how she loved blindly trusting people. Plus, it was addressed to her. Her full, utterly hated, name. Digory? Really?

Rebecca flipped the envelope and slid her finger beneath the flap, breaking the seal without a problem. "I'm ninety-nine percent sure it's the same, but if it makes you feel better…" She tugged the single card from its sheath. It was thick and firm, like all the others. Her psycho writer didn't cheap out on cardstock. She recognized the gold ink and swirling script. He was also consistent in his font choices. He should break it up a little. There was no law against interspersing a few variations. She cleared her throat before she began reading.

"'The Ruling Alphas of the North American Packs…'" She looked to Joseph. "The sender is a little crazy." When he frowned at her attempt at humor, she went back to reading. "'Demand.' Nothing new there. He's been demanding since day one."

"How long ago was that?"

Rebecca frowned and thought back. "I got the first one on my birthday a few weeks ago." She shrugged. "Anyway, they demand. Not 'cordially' this time, though. Demand I attend this 'Gathering' thing and then when I finish reading this summons…" That was new… she kept scanning the "summons," following along until she got to the bottom. "'You will be immediately transported to the Wolfson Hoooo…'"

The breeze suddenly picked up, whipping her with its force and assaulting her with pellets of dirt—she fucking hated dirt—as it encircled her. She clutched her backpack, fisting the water-resistant fabric. The strength of the air almost ripped it from her grasp, but she tightened her hold further. The world around her dimmed until darkness surrounded her. The wind still battered her body, shoving her this way and that, while the ground dropped from beneath her. Or did she rise?

Who cared? The ass was not on the floor. Period. There was no hard surface-to-ass connection.

It was as if she floated in a sea of black—and wasn't that all poetic.

Then, just as quick as the world disappeared, it returned with a bone-jarring, pain-inducing thump when the aforementioned ass collided with a rock-hard floor.

A floor that was polished to a mirror shine. Cream tiles with darker lines of deep brown and strands of white threaded throughout. The pale color was offset by splashes of black. A mosaic. She was sitting on a shiny cream and black mosaic.

The biggest change was the absence of dirt.

Where the fuck was the dirt? Panic slammed into her, hot and fierce, and it clung to her heart. Adrenaline poured into her veins while that good ol' fight or flight crawled into her body. She was all about flighting. Big time with the flighting.

13

The loud roar and whoosh of water yanked her attention from the floor to the stalls lining the wall to her right. Bathroom stalls. Right. She looked to her left and spied a bank of sinks. She was in a bathroom, a high-end, hoity-toity bathroom to be sure, but still a bathroom.

Great. She'd gone from forest to Toilet Land.

The jiggling of metal was followed by a scraping squeak and then one of the stall doors swung open. A woman strode out, high heels clicking and clacking on the marble floor.

If Rebecca weren't going crazy, she'd call the woman pretty. Okay, gorgeous.

But she was going crazy, which meant only three words flew from her mouth. "What the fucking fuck of all fucks?"

Okay, seven, but she should count it as three since all the fucking should be considered one word and then "what" was an important part of a sentence so she'd take "all" as her third word and...

What the fuck was she *thinking*?

"Oh." The woman's voice was tinkling yet seductive and oozed sex. One syllable and even Rebecca was thinking twice about her love of penises. "You're one of *them*."

"One of—"

The bathroom door swung open and a wolf trotted in. That was crazy enough, but then said wolf transformed. That was the only word for it. One second wolf, the next second very gorgeous, very human woman.

Rebecca squeaked, the dressed woman frowned, and the *naked* woman smirked.

Now would be a good time to pass out. Maybe when she woke up she would be back in the forest. On dirt. She fucking loved dirt.

CHAPTER THREE

Aidan crossed his legs and leaned against the wall outside one of the hotel's ballroom doors as he waited for the "festivities" to begin. Noise surrounded him, conference goers filing past, through the double doors. Their words formed a cacophony of noise that bounced off the marble flooring and walls. The hard surfaces amplified the sounds until the roar rang in his ears. The hotel was a picture of elegance that was wasted on a bunch of wolves who would be more at home in a forest than surrounded by opulence.

He didn't know why the Ruling Alphas held a Gathering every year. The concept of finding his mate was tempting, but unrealistic. Sure, the aforementioned Ruling Pair found their mate last year, and the Ruling Wardens had as well. Then there was the third Wickham sister Gabriella with those two Alphas…

He shook his head. Nah, it was a fluke. Maybe ten percent of the males who attended the Gathering found their mates. Alpha Pairs from across the country were required to attend, and now Warden Pairs were lumped in after that mess with Whitney Wickham and the Ruling Wardens.

Then there were the single wolves. They couldn't mate with humans, not like the Alphas and Wardens, but individual males and females couldn't resist the chance to party. What better way to mingle and meet others than on the Ruling Alphas' dime?

His phone vibrated in his pocket, drawing his attention, and he fished it out. He expected a text from his other—not necessarily better—Alpha half. There was no doubt Carson had been waylaid by yet another female looking for a good time. With Carson being the prettier of them, he constantly got hit on. Unfortunately, they had a place to be which meant Carson would have to take a pass on the female. He doubted that'd put her off though. When his partner shot down a female, she still walked away floating on air and half in love with the wolf.

Sighing, he swiped his thumb over the screen, smiling when the familiar background came into view. His family—him, his younger half-brother, and their dad—all shifted, while his brother attempted to swallow Aidan's head whole. Literally. Aidan had been a runt until puberty and his brother never let him forget it.

Another vibration and he tapped the text message icon. He scrolled through them, finding the newest first from Scarlet, the Ruling Alpha Mate:

The world is in chaos. Woman down! Save yourselves! Kidding. There are more crazed women than anticipated. Gathering disclaimer now includes any infectious diseases known to man. The women are from all corners of the Earth including remote villages in South America where bathing is optional.

What the hell? Aidan admitted he hadn't glanced at his phone when he woke, but what was she rambling about? The woman was a little unhinged, but…

He scrolled back to the previous one… *No sniffing butts? Penises?*

Aidan shook his head. Yeah, she'd lost it. A new message popped up, and this one came from Carson. Thank God, he about gave up on his partner.

Grab a beer. You won't believe this shit.

Aidan glanced at his watch. At noon? Fuck it. He pushed away from the wall and eased into the mass of bodies. The rumble of voices echoed around him, filling his ears with the rambling words. His wolf whined at the overwhelming sounds, but there wasn't much he could do about it. Until they got into the grand ballroom, and the Ruling Alphas called for quiet, the wolves were like high school kids, talking as loud as they possibly could and not caring about anyone else.

His fucking animal hated loud noise, these crowds, and especially hated strangers touching him. Ever since…

It'd taken hours, but the docs and nurses had eventually gotten him stitched back together. He rubbed his chest, wiping away the rising ache and pushing back the memory.

He moved closer to the bar he'd seen on his way downstairs. Positioned near the lobby, it was the perfect spot to snare a drink on the go. He was almost to the place of salvation when a sweet scent slammed into him, and a blur of brown caught his eye. It shouldn't have grabbed his attention. Plenty of wolves were brown, and quite a few of the attendees liked wandering around in their fur. The Ruling Alphas didn't give a damn about a person's shape as long as they followed orders.

So, yeah, brown and sweet and it raced along the wall and against the flow of traffic. His wolf whined and pawed him, urging him to follow that scent, but he rolled his eyes at the beast and kept moving toward his destination.

A low whimper reached his ears, one that was filled with fear. It rolled through the crowd, traveling on the vibrating air, and Aidan wondered why his animal singled out that one sound above the others. But it did. It found it and clutched it and snarled to turn his stubborn ass around and follow the aromas of crisp winter and ripe berries.

Groaning, Aidan turned and retraced his path. He pushed through the moving mass of bodies, ignoring the bestial grumbles that sounded in his wake. Each one started threatening as hell and then ended as abruptly as it'd begun.

Sometimes being bigger than everyone had its advantages.

Before long, conference attendees stepped out of the way, creating a widening path toward the wall. As soon as he got close enough, he drew the fresh scent into his lungs. It rose above the woodsy smell of the werewolves in attendance. It seemed to reach into him and sink into his bones.

Shit, he was getting all poetic.

He turned right, internally smiling when some of the weaker wolves practically ran in the opposite direction. Though, if he were telling the truth, even the weaker wolves were Alphas. Just not Alphas like *him*.

He dropped his attention to the ground, to the brown scrapings decorating the floor and the clumps of dirt that lay on the cream marble. Housekeeping was gonna be pissed. Those women were fierce, and even Aidan was a little afraid of them.

Following the person's scent and trail, he strode down the hall. He pushed people aside when they weren't paying close enough attention to get out of his way. The faster his quarry moved, the more insistent his beast became. It wanted to be with the source. Now. It wanted to be beside the person, wrap it in his arms, hold her close and…

Her.

Yes. Her.

The wolf knew what it wanted, and it craved the woman. The hint of tempting musk intermingling with the berries and sunshine should have immediately clued him in, but he had been distracted by the plethora of bodies surrounding him.

The female changed her path, turning left and down a side hallway, her steps grinding dirt into the plush patterned carpet. As he entered the new hall, he caught sight of a flash of brown and then she was gone with a quick right turn.

Aidan's cell phone vibrated, and he spared it a glance. Carson must've still been waiting, and the man was texting him. Increasing his pace, he hit reply.

Hunting. South hall.

They were surrounded by conference rooms, places meant to accommodate meetings between Alpha Pairs and Marked females. When she ducked into a room on the right, he knew there was one way in and one way out.

He jerked to a halt outside the door and breathed deeply, savoring the seductive scent. He wanted it, wanted to bathe in it and coat his skin. The wolf ached to roll in the aroma and let it cover every strand of fur.

A sign to the left of the door caught his attention, and he added to his text.

Bad Doggie meeting room.

Aidan rolled his eyes. The Ruling Alpha Mate and her idea of jokes.

Carson was quick to reply. *WTF?*

Yeah, he understood his partner's feelings. *Get here.*

With that final reply, he tucked his phone in his pocket and reached for the door. Aidan's skin rippled, his wolf lurking beneath the surface and ready to pounce. It was like a cat, crouched and prepared to leap when the moment was right. It wanted the woman on the other side of the door more than it'd ever wanted *anything.*

Which scared the shit out of him.

But that didn't keep him from gripping the handle and pressing the lever to disengage the catch. He tugged, and the panel swung toward him, granting him entrance, and more importantly, gifting him with more of that sugary scent. He drew the flavors in until they sank into his blood. The wolf howled in appreciation, urging Aidan to move into the space and hunt her.

Fur slid free of his pores and just as quickly sunk back into his skin. The animal wanted out, wanted to pursue her, but the beast also knew it was easier to talk to her without a wolf's snout.

There was something else in her flavors. Or rather there was something *missing* from her scent. She wasn't a wolf, but one hundred percent human. Which meant that, because she was at the Gathering, she was either Alpha Marked or Warden Born.

For the first time in his life, Aidan felt a hint of hope and... desire. Not a hard-on that was easily served by any woman who dropped to her knees. No, this was a soul-deep craving.

Aidan stepped into the room and scanned the interior. Tables and trios of chairs were scattered throughout the small area, the furniture setup specifically for Tests of Proximity. They were all very scheduled and rigid, specific times when Alpha Marked could sit with Alpha Pairs to determine if they were a match. The Ruling Alpha Mate described it as werewolf speed dating. *"Sniff? No burning marks? Next!"*

Honestly, it was good that structure was in place. He couldn't imagine what it'd be like if wolves were allowed to run rampant and pounce on every passing female. This kept everyone safe.

Well, everyone but the female he hunted. This chase was so far out of bounds it was ridiculous, but the animal inside him wouldn't let him break off his pursuit.

He let the door swing closed behind him. The loud scrape of metal on metal and the final echoing thunk of it latching bolted through the room. A low whimper followed on its heels, and he swung his attention toward the source. His quarry wasn't in sight, but that didn't worry him, or the wolf. They'd find her.

He took a step farther into the room, and her scent surrounded him. His cock twitched and hardened, not filling his jeans, but enough to make it uncomfortable to walk. No matter. This woman was the first female he'd wanted since… ever, honestly. He fucked plenty of women, but they'd always been after Carson. Aidan was always an afterthought to them. Which made him go through the motions rather than revel in the pleasure. He got off, but it was empty.

His wolf *would* have this female.

Aidan slowly made his way toward the back right corner of the room. The low, luring whimper had come from that direction, and he hadn't seen her scurry to another hiding place. With each step closer, his body burned hotter, cock pulsing with need and his hip… He rubbed his right hip, a burning throb taking up residence the nearer he got to his prey.

Aidan froze in place, ceasing his travels as he stroked that spot. His dick ached, but that was because he wanted to fuck the woman he chased. The rest of him was healthy and strong. Wolves were hardy, and their very nature kept them free of illness. He hadn't gotten into a brawl in at least a week and even then he would have healed in a day.

So there was no reason for him to have a random, ever increasing pain as he tracked the woman. Unless… He gulped. No. *No.*

If an Alpha Pair found their Marked, their mate, then the woman's Mark would burn and pulse. Which, in turn, caused that same area to throb on the men's bodies.

So there was only one reason he'd have a painfully hard dick that had him ready to blow at any moment, and a burning sensation on his hip that refused to be extinguished.

She was there. His mate, their mate.

Aidan's cell phone vibrated, the buzz slicing the silence, and the woman gasped. She kept quiet at least, nearly soundless, but his wolf's ears picked it up.

He looked at his phone once again, only the words on the screen didn't catch his attention. No, it was the scars decorating his hands and arms. Some were hardly visible, time having made them blend with his natural color, while others were raised and stark white against his tanned skin.

The ageless unease that lurked in the back of his mind rushed forward. He was certain she belonged to them, but he wasn't sure he could survive if she turned from him and sought out Carson like every other woman they'd enjoyed.

24

He wasn't much to look at, not with the damage he'd sustained all those years ago. He hoped—

The grating of the door hit him a brief moment before Carson's voice reached him. "Yo, fucker, we're late and you know those guys—"

He hadn't torn his attention from his mate's hiding place so when she squeaked and jumped from her spot behind the table to bolt from him, it was easy to snare her.

Aidan snatched her to him, hooking his arm around her waist and halting her run for freedom. He yanked her against his body, molding her back to his front, and his cock took notice of their proximity. The burning on his hip became a full body ache to have her beneath him—he spared a glance for Carson—beneath them.

She was all plump curves and silken skin. The scents of the forest coated her flesh, but he delved deeper to that sweet aroma that had him following her. Yes, it was there. Perfection.

"Aidan!" Carson yelled at him, but it was as if it were at a distance. His entire focus remained on the female—on her deep brown hair that held shades of red in its depths. On the roundness of her ass as it pressed against his cock, the curve of her waist as he held her captive, the way her abundant breasts rested atop his forearm.

He wanted to see her face, look into her eyes and trace her features with his gaze. His wolf howled for her, demanding he claim her now, right this second. But that wasn't how things worked. It wasn't how the process progressed, and he'd never hated laws more.

"What the fu—" Carson gasped and he knew what his partner was experiencing.

Uncontrollable want and burning need.

The woman he held captive fought him, kicking and scratching, and he smiled. She wasn't a weak female. Then again, one destined for Alphas couldn't be a wilting flower. She had to be strong to stand up to men who led a pack.

Unable to hold back his curiosity, he spun her around. He shifted his hold until her front met his, and his arm was secure around her back. Shining blue eyes collided with his, fear and panic filling them. He should try to soothe her, release her and calm her obvious terror.

Instead, he noted the gentle slope of her nose, her heart-shaped face, and her plump lips. He wanted to capture them with his own and dive into a passionate kiss. He'd taste her, soothe her, and then take her.

She... did not feel the same.

She screamed so loudly it nearly shattered his eardrums. Then she asked the most absurd question imaginable.

"Are you an alien, too?" Her voice rose with the last word, and if he weren't so enamored with the tinkling quality of the syllables, he would have laughed. Instead, his cock throbbed.

"No, I'm a werewolf." His words were matter of fact and blunt.

She shivered in his hold, and her feminine musk drifted to him. She was aroused, or at least feeling a bit of desire, and she was focused on him. At his scars and crooked nose and the way his eyes were the deep yellow of his wolf twenty-four/seven.

"Werewolves aren't real," she whispered. "Can you be an alien instead? That would be better. An alien would be

26

better." She nodded, her fallen curls hiding her eyes. He brushed them from her face, and she didn't flinch from him. If anything, the scent of her cream increased. "You know what's even better than aliens? Passing out. Can I do that now? I'd like to do that now."

Another nod from her and he grinned. She was perfect. A little bit crazy and gorgeous as hell.

"Tell me your name first." His wolf filled his voice, and she gave a low whimper, but it wasn't one of fear. No, not a hint of fright tinged the sound. It was all arousal.

"Rebecca."

"Rebecca." He tested the name on his tongue, savoring the syllables. "Pass out, Rebecca. I have you."

"Thanks so much."

She truly had been waiting for permission because the moment she said the last word, she went limp in his arms. Her head lolled back, and Carson was there, cupping her skull in his hand.

"Aidan?" Carson's voice was rough. "Is she…"

"Yes." There was no doubt in his mind. The burning need, the wolf's reaction to her. Yes, she was theirs. "She's—"

"Unhand the woman!" A familiar voice cut into their conversation, and Aidan groaned. "Penises better not have entered orifices! Or teeth!" Scarlet spun and snapped at the Gathering organizer. "Send a new text. No teeth." Aidan's cell phone buzzed with a text message. Then they were the focus of the Ruling Alpha Mate once again. "Let her go."

"She's ours," Aidan snarled, and Carson added his own growl.

Instead of being afraid of their combined anger, the woman snorted. "What. Ever. Emmett and Levy felt her appearance and also informed me she has no idea what she's doing here. So hand her over for orientation and then we'll see what we can see."

"She's ours." This time it was Carson, and the male sounded even more threatening than Aidan ever had.

Scarlet glared. "She'll go through tests and meetings like every other woman here, boys. She needs to understand everything before she's shoved into our world. Every year there are Marked who are dragged here by the Wardens and they have *no idea* what they're in for. There are even more women this year because of the Warden Born. Do you think she'd have ended up in this room if she knew? Don't you think she would have checked in like any other Marked woman and actually *showered* before coming downstairs?"

Aidan was reminded of the dirt covering his female, the smudges that lined her cheeks and the soil that covered her clothing. He accepted that Scarlet's assumptions were correct. Rebecca had been brought to the Gathering through a Warden's summoning, and she didn't know about the wolves, Marks, or what awaited her when she awoke.

And... she needed to know before things went further, before he and Carson stripped her bare and claimed her as their own. He didn't like it, but it was necessary. He hoped she'd accept them when she knew the truth.

"Where"—he cleared his throat and pushed back the emotions crowding his chest—"where should we take her?"

28

CHAPTER FOUR

Rebecca stared at the three women surrounding her. They'd been there from the moment she'd opened her eyes and still hadn't left her alone.

And alone would be a good thing. If she were by herself, she'd find a way to escape the crazies standing before her as well as those who lurked on the other side of the door.

Who knew they had an asylum that held thousands of people who all had the *same* delusion? It was one for the record books.

Even worse, they were her cousins. Blood relatives. Was Rebecca going to drink the Kool-Aid and suddenly join them in Crazy Town?

"Sooo…" Rebecca raised her eyebrows and looked to Scarlet, their "Ruling Alpha Mate." Whatever that was. Rebecca didn't wanna know. "I haven't seen you three since we were kids. I mean, we last got together before the great *Family Implosion of Doom* during the last family reunion."

Scarlet rolled her eyes. "Yeah, well, it was your mom's fault. She was all—"

"Focus," Gabby snapped at Scarlet and then returned her attention to Rebecca. "Go ahead. We know you have questions."

Questions? Right. She shook her head. "To recap. Werewolves are real." All three women nodded. "And this is the annual Gathering." Another set of nods. "And women

29

who have either a weird scar tattoo thing or who are meant to be with magic werewolves"—*holy shit, magic is real*—"are summoned here with aforementioned magic." More nods. "And I was dragged here by magic because I hadn't shown up yet?"

"Right," Whitney, the quietest of the three responded.

"Which means I have a Mark thingy, or I'll glow in the dark and get a shit-ton of Mark thingies like Whitney." Rebecca gulped when they all gave the same nods. "I would prefer aliens."

Whitney patted Rebecca's arm. "I know, but it's real, werewolves are real. The existence of werewolves, Marked, and Warden Born are as old as time."

"It could be a mistake," she interjected hopefully.

"No." Scarlet shook her head. "The mojo-wielding idiots may not have done things exactly right, but they aren't wrong about getting the women here. You just didn't end up in the right place here. You see, the ballroom is set up so that…" Scarlet gestured behind her and Rebecca peered around her cousins to find more clumps of women throughout the massive room. Small groups surrounded single, panic-stricken women, and she imagined they were all receiving the same news.

Werewolves were real, and they were meant to mate with one.

Mate…

"You realize I don't have a Mark thing. I mean, I know my body, right?" Scarlet and Gabby had flashed their Marks during show and tell so she knew what she was looking for. But she also knew every scarred, taut inch of her body and

30

nary a Mark was to be seen. Just burns, and she was thankful those were easily covered with clothing. "And there's no scar thing." Other scars, but they were twisted masses of skin and tissue. Not the pretty swirls that decorated her cousins.

"The thing about *that* is…" Scarlet began again, and Gabby picked up the end of the sentence.

"You wouldn't be here without one. If you don't have a Mark"—Gabby raised her eyebrows and Rebecca shook her head—"then you're meant for a pair of Wardens. Which, I mean, is kinda cool. When I mated Berke and Jack, I only got awesome sex and those two constantly in my head. Whitney got super powers and this glowing thing when she gets pissed. I mean, it usually comes right before she whips out her power-dick, but whatever."

Said woman suddenly glowed as she glared at Gabby.

"*Any*-way." Scarlet clapped her hands twice. "Back on track, people. Gabby, quit antagonizing Whitney. When she burns your ass—again—I will totally forbid your mates from rubbing your butt." Gabby shrugged and Scarlet continued. "Or fucking it."

"Hey now, that's a low blow," Gabby whined.

"Uh…" Rebecca swallowed back her panic. "Berke and Jack? Two men?" Did they leave something out? Screw it, she'd ask. "Did you leave something out of this lovely delusion you've drawn me into?"

It was kinda nice if she ignored the werewolf part and enjoyed the fancy hotel, forced vacation thing.

"Oh. Yeah. You boink two guys. Never one. Single wolves boink single wolves, but Alpha and Warden Pairs need a non-furry human woman to balance them. Otherwise"—

Scarlet waved her hands in the air as if they were cars and then rammed her fists into each other—"boom. Madness, and in the case of Alphas, lots of blood ensues." Scarlet's eyes widened. "Which reminds me. Are you super sure you don't have a Mark? Anywhere? Because those guys you met—"

Guys… She'd met two and only got a good look at one of them. He was all kinds of tall, dark, and do me now. "Yeah?"

"They kinda sorta think you're their mate but you can't be their mate if you don't have a Mark. So, if we could take an itty-bitty peek to make sure you don't—"

"No." She shut her cousin down before she voiced the rest of the question. It didn't matter if they were family, there were parts of her she didn't want anyone to see.

"But they think… And…" Scarlet frowned. "You don't feel the need to climb them like a mountain and beg them to plant their flags? I mean, I know Aidan isn't much to look at, but—"

A growl built in Rebecca's throat and vibrated the air around her. "He's gorgeous."

Scarlet's eyes widened. "That was kind of scary awesome. Gorgeous?"

"Yes," Rebecca snapped.

"Right. You might be Marked and just not know it. Maybe in your vagina? Especially since you think Aidan with all his freakishly large size and, you know, Land-o-Scarring is hot. And they wanna hump your leg like a fire hydrant." Scarlet nodded to reaffirm her statement. "Like, hard core."

Yeah, well, Rebecca felt the urge to do her own kind of humping though hers was more like rubbing all over him. Her right hip tingled, warming, and a sliver of arousal slithered into her veins. She'd reacted the same way when in that small room with that guy—Aidan?—and it intensified when the other man entered.

Rebecca grimaced and shook her head. "They're hot." So friggin' hot. "But I'd know if I had a Mark. Really."

Her cousins exchanged a speaking look, and it appeared they had a silent conversation before focusing on Rebecca again.

Scarlet spoke, and she figured it made sense. She was the eldest and ruler-type person. "Okay, but since you're new, it might be a good idea to have a guard or two."

Rebecca huffed. "A babysitter?"

"Well, okay, fine. A babysitter." Scarlet waved her hand. "I'm ninety-nine percent sure a few other Wickham cousins are gonna pop up. I mean, we were really close in age at the family reunion, right? You were three, I was four? We were little, but I remember you and your sisters. If any of them were Warden Born, their happy asses were automagically hauled here. And they won't have any clue like you and—" A shout had them all turning toward the main doors. Two massive men—probably werewolves and *not* aliens—carefully dragged a woman into the room. "And it'd be great to not have to worry about you." Scarlet turned to her again. "I mean, can you be trusted not to pull a gun on anyone?"

Rebecca tilted her head to the side, thinking about what her backpack held. Thank God she hadn't released it when she was hauled through that dark, scary as hell place. "Gun? No, I don't have a gun."

Bear repellant was a different story, and it'd probably work. Bears were big and had fur. All the men she'd seen here were massive and sometimes had fur. It'd work.

All three women deflated, releasing relieved sighs.

"Good, that's real good," Scarlet spoke again. "So I'm going to release you to Aidan and Carson."

"Carson?"

"The other guy. Not quite as big, no freaky scars—"

Something inside Rebecca snapped. "Stop talking about Aidan that way."

Scarlet rocked back on her heels. "Right, right. You're going with them. They're an Alpha Pair, so they have a big-assed suite. You can stay there until you find your mate or the Gathering ends. Whichever comes first. They're good guys. Uh…" Scarlet scrunched her nose. "Can I call them scary? Because, really, they are."

Rebecca leveled a glare on Scarlet. "I can see why the Twynhams and Wickhams don't talk anymore."

"Hey, now." Whitney spoke up. "Let's not bring that drama-llama here. We already have enough. Our parents and grandparents were the ones who had problems, but that doesn't mean we have to. This will give us a chance to get to know one another without our families interfering." Whitney reached out and squeezed Rebecca's hand. "We didn't have cousins growing up and I think it'd be awesome to have one. Maybe we could have dinner while you're here. I know you're still reeling from all this, but you could sit down with our mates and learn a little more about us all without this madness."

Yeah, Rebecca felt the same. She had her sisters, Lorelei and Paisley, but they hadn't had cousins growing up. "Sure, that sounds good."

"Great!" Gabby clapped her hands. "Let's get you to your matching mountains and then we can try and keep the rest of these women from neutering any of the wolves."

With that, Gabby snared Rebecca's hand and hauled her from the couch. Before she was dragged away, she snatched up her dirty backpack. "Do you think I could get a shower? Or clothes?"

Or at least a washing machine and a sink so she didn't reek of the forest.

Gabby smirked at her. "Oh, Hunks One and Two will take care of ya."

Rebecca groaned. "You're making it sound like something it's not. They're hot, but if what you say is true, then..." There's nothing between them.

Gabby jolted to a halt and grabbed both of Rebecca's hands. "Listen to me. I know what the Wardens believe, and I know there are all kinds of rules and laws hanging around. But Whitney, who didn't have a Mark, found her mates with Emmett and Levy. If they want you this bad and you want them just as much, then there's probably someone else who got things wrong. Don't push them away because of what all these people say."

"You're one of these people."

Gabby shrugged. "Yeah, but I'm awesome-er, so I don't count."

They resumed their trek toward the main set of doors. The moment they stepped into the hallway, Aidan and who had to be Carson jumped in their path. Neither touched Rebecca, but she sensed their need to lay their hands on her. She felt the same desire, the urge to stroke Aidan's skin and run her fingers through Carson's wavy hair.

Gabby proceeded with introductions, but Rebecca remembered Aidan's embrace and the deep rumble of Carson's voice. "Aidan Hall and Carson Holland, Garden Ridge, Illinois Alpha Pair, let me introduce you to Rebecca Twynham. Also known as a Wickham cousin."

"Cousin?" That did not sound like a deep rumble. No, Carson squeaked like a mouse.

"Yes, the family had a falling out when we were young, but she's our cousin and we've all agreed she might be more comfortable staying with you two for the weekend."

"She's ours. It'll be longer than a weekend." Carson's voice was filled with unyielding conviction, and his eyes went from a gorgeous chocolate brown to a bright amber. An amber similar to Aidan's. Like a wolf. A wolf's eyes or a werewolf's eyes and holy cow it finally slammed home that she wasn't surrounded by aliens, but honest to God werewolves.

She focused on his words, on the blatant proclamation, and her heart stuttered. She wanted his statement to be true so, so badly. Because even if she weren't the type of girl to snare such hotties, she'd take them without hesitation.

But… "I, uh, don't think I am. Because… You see… I don't have…"

Gabby placed her hand in Rebecca's and squeezed. "What Rebecca is trying to say is she's not Marked."

*

The world around Carson ceased to exist the moment Rebecca stepped from the Grand Ballroom. Hell, he hardly noticed Gabby's presence at her side. His entire focus was on Rebecca and Rebecca alone. Their mate had emerged, and now they could get to the matter of claiming her. Sure, some wooing might have to happen since she knew nothing of wolves, but he planned on sinking into her heat as deep and often as possible.

He was more than up for it now. If she were willing…

Damn it, his cock seemed to get even harder and fuck if his hip didn't tingle and throb in time with his heart. His wolf caught her scent and howled in approval, prepared to claim the small human woman as their own. She was a tiny thing, short and curved in all the right places. He couldn't wait to run his hands through her hair and fist the strands as she sucked his dick. Yes, as soon as he got enough of her pussy and ass, he'd have her wrap those plump lips around his shaft. He'd beg if that's what it took.

When it came to Rebecca, he'd gladly drop to his knees if it meant being close to her. And naked. It wouldn't be worth it unless they were nude and sweaty and…

Then Gabby's words cut through his fantasies and sunk into his brain. "Wait, what?" He shook his head. "She's…"

"Ours." Aidan's voice was flat and emotionless, but Carson knew better. His partner was holding his wolf back by a thread.

Gabby gave him a kind smile. "I understand, but…"

The heavy weight of Aidan's gaze slammed into him, but he kept his attention trained on the women before him. Aidan wanted him to fix things, but some things were broken beyond repair. He craved Rebecca like no other, but if she didn't have a Mark...

His wolf howled its objection and scraped his flesh from inside out. Normally the beast expressed his complaints by attacking Carson's arms and forcing his hands to shift. But today, it scratched him in an altogether different spot. His right hip. As before, an ache enveloped the area, the warmth and tingling sensation sinking into his blood and moving to encircle his rapidly hardening shaft. The animal dragged its claws, bringing his attention to the location.

When Rebecca moved her hand and rubbed the same area on her own body, he realized he didn't give a damn about Gabby's words. Rebecca had a Mark. She had to have one. He couldn't accept any other truth.

Maybe Rebecca was simply unwilling to accept her new reality. Maybe she was nervous about craving two men she'd just met. Hell, he didn't give a damn *why* she denied having a Mark as long as she was going to spend the weekend with them.

Carson stepped forward and snared her free hand. Slowly, carefully, he brought it to his lips. He rotated her wrist and placed a tender kiss to her palm. "Hello."

Rebecca's eyes widened, her pupils growing in size until they almost obliterated the sparkling blue of her irises. Her chest rose and fell as she panted and fought for breath and the seductive, musky scent of her arousal surrounded them.

Oh, their little mate wanted them. There was no doubt about that fact.

"I can see I'm not needed," Gabby's voice interfered, but he didn't bother tearing his gaze from Rebecca. "The family wants to have dinner with you three. Tonight? Eight?"

Aidan grunted his assent while Carson nodded. He couldn't tear his gaze from Rebecca.

"Okay, then. See ya." Gabby patted Rebecca, and it took everything in him not to snarl at the woman for touching the woman who belonged to him—to them. She was his mate's cousin; pissing her off probably wasn't a good idea.

The moment Gabby left their immediate area, Aidan was there, his massive body behind their small mate. Carson watched her reaction to the other Alpha. Rather than shy away from his bulk, she leaned against the large male. Unlike every woman they'd ever encountered, she sought shelter in his Alpha partner. That proved once again she was the one for them.

A low grumble, one that didn't come from Carson's or Aidan's beasts, reached his ears, and a pink blush stole over Rebecca's cheeks.

"Hungry?" He raised his eyebrows, hoping she said yes. They could feed her, take care of her. That pleased his wolf and the animal ceased his torment and changed its focus. Now it was intent on herding her toward the nearest restaurant.

Rebecca nodded and then grimaced. "Yeah, but I could use a shower and a change of clothes first. Something other than"—she glanced down and picked at her shorts, sending a cascade of dirt drifting to the ground—"mud *chic*."

Another way for them to care for her. "We'll go to our suite. We can order room service. While you clean up, we'll see about getting you some clothes."

A rumbling growl came from Aidan and Carson felt his wolf answer the sound. Images of a naked, wet Rebecca filled his mind, and he recognized those same thoughts in Aidan's. It was great to almost share a brain.

Rebecca squeaked as his partner slid his arm around her waist to hug her close. That earned them another squeak and damn if that wasn't a sexy sound.

Carson crowded her as well, easing forward until she was captured between their bodies. She pulled back from him the tiniest bit, and he leaned toward her. She wouldn't escape them. Her warmth invaded him as did the flavors of her need. He couldn't wait to taste her. His hip burned now, heating and pulsing, practically screaming that Rebecca belonged to them.

"Um…" The vibrations of her single word snaked along his spine, and his gums ached with the need to bare his fangs and sink them into her shoulder. It wouldn't claim her, not truly, but it'd be a good warning to other wolves. "You guys are, um…" She swallowed and he traced the line of her neck with his gaze. "You're kinda, you know." She wiggled and Aidan groaned. Carson's came right on its heels.

"Yeah, we are. You're so damned gorgeous." Carson stroked her cheek.

"Ours." His partner nuzzled her neck, and he smiled when she tilted her head to the side.

"And we're both imagining you wet and naked." His lips spread further, widening his smile when Aidan scraped her skin with a fang and she sucked in a rough breath.

"You heard what Gabby said. You should"—she tilted her head even farther, giving Aidan more room, and he'd never been jealous of his friend before this moment—"you should

40

never stop doing that." She released the words in a breathless rush. "Ever."

Carson stilled, his limbs freezing, and a slow realization crept through him. Rebecca was responding to Aidan, begging him for more. She'd leaned against him, not pushing his partner away when he'd pulled her against him.

When Carson stepped up to her, did the same, she eased back for the barest of moments. Disappointment speared him, the reversal of roles slamming into him like a sledgehammer, and he backed away from her.

"We should get her to our suite, Aidan." He didn't withhold the annoyed growl in his tone.

His partner raised his head from their mate's shoulder and shot him a confused look, but he ignored the expression. Rebecca took a jerky step back, further pushing against Aidan, and shook her head, eyes now bright blue instead of mostly black as her arousal vanished.

"Oh." She squeezed her eyes tight and then reopened them. "Yeah, a shower and food would be great."

With those words from her lips, Carson spun on his heel and headed into the mass of moving bodies. He glanced over his shoulder and confirmed Rebecca and Aidan were behind him. His partner ensured no one bothered her or impeded their travels. Rebecca's hand rested on Aidan's as he clutched her right shoulder. It was an awkward position, but it didn't seem to matter to her.

Another Alpha bumped into Carson, clipping his shoulder, and Carson snarled at the male, baring his teeth. The wolf pushed them forward without hesitation, ready to take on the asshole. It was pissed as hell, angry Rebecca seemed to prefer Aidan to him.

41

Aidan was gruff and large and scarred while Carson wasn't and...

The other Alpha scurried away while bile rose hot and fast up his throat. It burned him, and he quickly swallowed it. Had he truly gone there with his thoughts? Allowed his mind to make that comparison?

It had. Oh, God, it had.

Carson increased his pace, uncaring if Aidan and Rebecca followed. He had a responsibility to ensure her safety and calm, but that didn't mean he had to be with her every moment. He'd get her to their suite, and then he'd... be anywhere other than there.

He pressed the elevator button, pushing over and over until the damn thing finally returned to their level.

Others approached when the doors slid open, but his glare was enough to dissuade them. Rebecca preceded Aidan, and as his partner passed, Aidan sent a mental message into his mind.

What's up with you?

"I'm fine." He didn't want that connection with Aidan. Not right now. He didn't want to feel his partner's joy at touching Rebecca.

You're not.

Carson spared a look for their mate, or rather Aidan's mate since he didn't think the woman really wanted Carson, and noted her nervous tension. "I'm. Fine. Let's get her to the suite."

Not their suite. *The* suite.

Aidan's gaze was crushing as the elevator rose. It remained when they walked down the wide hallway to their room and even as they entered their spacious suite. Their rooms didn't compare to the size of the Ruling Alphas' or the Ruling Wardens', but it was big enough for their triad.

Not that they were a triad. Maybe Gabby hadn't been lying. His wolf howled for Rebecca, but if she didn't want Carson, how could she be theirs?

They all strode into their home away from home and Carson couldn't care less about the polished marble floors, the plush carpets, the comfortable furniture, or the tasteful decorations. The view he'd coveted and bargained for when making their reservations didn't hold any appeal. In a few hours, he'd gone from riding high and craving Rebecca to dipping low and… craving Rebecca.

The wolf and his body would get over it.

Aidan was still holding their mate's hand. No, he needed to banish the word from his mind. He was holding *Rebecca's* hand.

"Why don't you show her the bathroom? I'll call for some clothes, and then I'm gonna get outta here." He ignored the snappish words.

Aidan furrowed his brow and stared at him. *Where are you going? We need to be here for our mate. She needs to get used to us so we can—*

"I've got things to do." He overrode his partner's telepathic speech. "I'll see you later." He nodded toward Rebecca. "You should show her the shower."

He presented the duo with his back. He didn't need to see them disappear behind the spare bedroom's door. Not when he realized he'd never follow them. Let Aidan get his lust sated by the gorgeous woman. How many times had they shared a woman who'd shied from Aidan? It was only fair it'd eventually happen in reverse. Carson just didn't think it'd happen so soon, or with a woman he wanted to claim as his own—as theirs. He didn't think he'd ever be jealous of Aidan and the life he'd lived.

And yet… Carson was.

CHAPTER FIVE

Something changed. Or had it? Rebecca wasn't sure. Hell, so many things had rearranged and shifted in the last few hours that she didn't know which way was up, or how to get to the nearest bed, naked with Aidan and Carson.

Man, that sounded like a really, really good idea.

Regardless, one second she was hot for Aidan and spying Carson. Then she was passed out and *OMF-ingG* she found out werewolves were real. Then more hot for Aidan *and* Carson, and then it was as if Carson flipped a switch, and he was as cold as ice to her.

Did the guy have IPS or something? Irritable Penis Syndrome was a real thing, even if doctors refused to accept its existence. Coincidentally, most of those doctors had penises so...

She followed Aidan into a guestroom, noting the space looked like any other hotel across the country. Well, a high-end, expensive as hell hotel. A massive bed occupied the center of the room, the comforter tasteful and looking comfortable as all get out. Beautifully carved bedside tables flanked the mattress, and a large flat-screen television was mounted on one wall.

"This way," Aidan murmured and he turned left, leading her toward an open doorway.

She followed him, ogling his ass while she had the chance. She also took in his thick thighs, tapered waist, and broad shoulders. He was beastly power on human legs. Staring at him, spying scars, she could see how others were intimidated or turned off, but Rebecca saw past it all. She saw a man—or rather a werewolf—who was over six feet of tightly controlled strength. It was apparent he easily held that power in check, and she sensed he could hurt someone without breaking a sweat. Yet he'd only use it if he had no other option.

In her heart, she felt as if a kitten lived inside him, one coated in matted fur and a hissing exterior, but still a kitten at heart.

Whereas Carson… She shook her head. She didn't know about him. She didn't know what he wanted, which made her not know what *she* wanted.

Aidan flicked the light on, pulling her from her thoughts. "Here's the bathroom. Jacuzzi tub, stand-up shower." He gestured to the left. "There's shampoo, conditioner, and soap here for you." He eased the door toward him. "A robe to tug on when you're done. We should have something for you to wear soon."

The words insinuated he was about to leave and yet he stayed put, his copper eyes burning into hers. That was something she noticed about him. She hadn't met too many werewolves, but the few she'd encountered had "normal" colored eyes whereas Aidan's were always the yellow-orange of his wolf.

So, instead of allowing him to leave, instead of stepping away, she moved forward, easing into his personal space. He didn't move, didn't even twitch when her clothing brushed his. She didn't plaster their bodies together no matter how much she wished to feel his heat. She'd recognized his earlier arousal, the thick length of him pressed against her back. He wanted her, and she'd reveled in his desire.

46

Now she hoped she could talk instead of touching him with want burning through them both.

She reached for him, slowly bringing her hand to cup his cheek. His breath caught and then he nuzzled her, those yellowed eyes drifting closed as he rubbed his rough cheek over her skin. Aidan pressed a soft kiss to her palm, much like Carson had fifteen minutes ago. Then his lids fluttered open, and he stared at her.

She ran her fingers over his cheek. "Why are your eyes like this? Why are they always the yellow of your wolf?" Aidan stiffened and his muscles tensed, body shifting as if he were about to move away. "No, I'm not trying to be mean." She dropped the bag she'd clutched like a lifeline since she'd been transported to the hotel. "I want to understand. I'm curious."

He looked away from her, his attention shifting to the opposite wall. "It bothers people." He bit off the words.

"Because it's your beast all the time?"

"Yes, our animal comes out, pushes through, when we're feeling heightened emotions. Anger." He glanced at her, the yellow glowing a hint brighter than before. "Lust."

That brought a blush to her cheeks. She'd definitely been lusting after them.

"But why are you so on edge like this? I mean, I assume it's because…" She let her words trail off as emotional pain coated his features.

"I… When I was younger… The wolf is always on guard because…"

Rebecca sensed a deep pain that lived within him, and she was quick to quiet his words. "Maybe we can talk about it later." She plucked at her shirt, dust blowing into the air. "I could really use a shower and then food. We'll sit and get to know each other after dinner?"

His relief was palpable, easily visible when his shoulders slumped and tension left his body. She knew he would have told her. He obviously didn't want to, but he would have. She ached for the pain he must have experienced, and she wondered if the hurt in his heart had something to do with the scars marring his skin.

"I mean, I don't have a Mark, but that doesn't mean we can't be friends while I'm here, right? We could—"

She'd never seen anyone move so fast. One moment there was air between them and the next she sat on the counter, Aidan's hips between her legs and his fingers tangled in her hair.

"*Mine.*" He snarled the single word and his eyes truly glowed, shining in the bright light. This was the difference between his typical yellow and his beast's appearance. *This.* He fisted her strands, using them to control her movements, and he forced her to meet his gaze. "You. Are. Mine." Another snarl, but it was cut off by his kiss.

But not just a kiss. No, it was a possession, a taking and claiming. He put his mark on her with his lips, teeth, and tongue. He delved into her mouth, and his flavors exploded over her taste buds.

She moaned and sagged against him, enjoying his dominance. She'd never gone for men who took charge and ran over her, but this… was delicious. She let him take what he desired while giving him everything she had. Her body reacted to his closeness, his scent surrounding her and his

48

flavors overwhelming her tongue. Her nipples pebbled, hardening within her bra while her center warmed and ached with the desire to be touched.

It'd never been like this with a guy. Ever. Encounters had been lukewarm at best. Sure, she came when with others, but Aidan made her feel like she could reach her peak through his kiss alone.

He growled against her and pulled away enough to nip her lower lip before delving into her once again. She wanted that and more. Much, much more. That spot on her hip warmed and pulsed, adding to the heat between her thighs. She wanted him there, craved his touch, his possession as he slid into her. She ached to writhe against him as he gave her pleasure and she hopefully gave him just as much in return.

She... wanted it all with Aidan. And even Carson despite his shift in attitude.

And yet... she couldn't because she wasn't Marked. For the first time in her life, she wished for another scar, another mark that overlaid the twisted flesh on her torso.

Rebecca tore her mouth from Aidan's, turning her head when he attempted to continue their passionate kiss.

"Stop." She hardly recognized her own voice, but he complied the moment the single word left her.

He pressed his forehead to her shoulder, panting and fighting for air while she did the same. She still thrummed with arousal, the pleasure of his touch slithering throughout her body. But giving in would be a mistake. One she wouldn't emotionally recover from. She could lose herself to Aidan and, by extension, Carson.

"I'm sorry." The words were garbled, but discernable.

"There's nothing to be sorry about. I don't think it's a good idea to…" *Get attached to you both.*

"It's a wonderful idea, but I shouldn't try to fuck you on the fucking bathroom counter." Aidan pulled back and cupped her cheeks, encouraging her to meet his gaze. "You're worth more than that, Rebecca." He gave her a gentle kiss, one meant to reassure and not send them spiraling into another whirlwind of lips, tongue, and teeth. "God, you're a temptation, and you sure as hell deserve a bed, sweet words." He sighed. "And a prettier face than mine."

Now Rebecca growled. Everyone had scars, issues that lingered whether they were physical or emotional. She had a little of both and imagined Aidan was the same. Carson… It seemed like his lurked in his heart. Part of her wanted to ferret them out and heal him. Then she remembered it wasn't her job. She wasn't theirs and… But did she have to belong to them to be a decent person?

No.

So, she'd try. Maybe. But she would wait until after her shower.

"Aidan?" He hummed in reply but didn't say anything. "You're gorgeous. Scars or not, you know you're hot. So quit fishing."

"I'm not—"

Rebecca narrowed her eyes and struck a cocky man where it hurt. "You sound like a girl."

That had him barking out a laugh, and the smile transformed his face from a brooding werewolf to a happy kid. Who had a dimple. That was so wrong.

"You're never going to be boring, are you?" The grin remained in place. As did the dimple.

"Nope." She shook her head and reminded herself of their temporary arrangement. She also drove the point home to him as well. "I can promise you a weekend of me being a pain in the butt."

"Rebecca…" Her name was a warning, but was cut off by Carson's shout.

"Aidan, what's taking so long?" Carson sounded annoyed, and Aidan sighed.

"Lemme see what he wants. Enjoy your shower. What do you want to eat? Burgers and fries? Steak?" He froze for a moment. "You're not a vegetarian, are you?" His tone was filled with utter dread, and she couldn't withhold her laugh.

"Hell, no. I'll take a burger, medium."

"Okay." He pressed one last, lingering kiss to her lips and then he was gone, striding through the bathroom door and out of sight.

She heard the soft click of the bedroom door swinging shut and hopped down from the counter. It took her seconds to turn on the shower and then strip off her mud-caked clothing. She was never going hiking again. Ever. Her wolves could get in touch with nature while she sat in a lounge chair in the shade of a massive oak with a screwdriver in hand. Orange juice was good for her, after all.

Her wolves. She shook her head. When she thought of her wolves, Aidan and Carson immediately sprung to mind. It didn't matter how many times she reminded herself they didn't belong to her, she ached to have them.

Stepping into the shower, she placed her hand in the spray and welcomed the heat. Sighing, she eased beneath the raining water and moaned. This was what she needed, and she ignored the part of her that screamed Aidan and Carson were what she needed as well.

*

Cock hard and ready to burst through his jeans, Aidan headed toward Carson, making sure to pull Rebecca's bedroom door shut. He wanted to leave it open and sneak a peek, but that'd be a total dick move.

Maybe he should go back...

He fisted his hands and took a deep breath, willing his body to calm and banish the burning need coursing through his veins. Of course, inhaling brought him more of Rebecca's delicious scent and his wolf urged him to return to her. The handful of kisses wasn't enough.

He knew he couldn't claim her fully but one little nip and others would—

"What the fuck? Took long enough. I ordered her clothes twenty minutes ago." Carson's voice held more than a bit of annoyance.

It sure as shit hadn't been twenty minutes. If he'd taken that much time, he would have already claimed their lush Rebecca.

"What the fuck? Fuck you, man." He snarled at his partner. He didn't know what crawled up the man's ass, but it needed to work its way out.

Carson paced from one end of the living room to the other, and Aidan noticed most of the furniture was haphazardly shoved aside. Hell, some of the chairs were overturned rather than nudged out of the way. Aidan breathed deep once again, but this time he focused on pushing back everything related to Rebecca and centered his attention on his partner.

Rage, hurt, and sadness filled his friend's scent.

"What's your damage, Carson?"

Carson glared at him and snarled, but didn't halt his pattern.

Screw that. They had had their share of fights through the years, but they'd never shied from the confrontations. Carson had always been quick to yell at him, and he was as quick to yell back. This silent treatment bullshit wasn't going to fly.

Aidan strode toward his partner and stepped into the man's path. "What's your problem? Other than her missing Mark, what's got you so pissed?"

Carson jolted to a stop and deepened his glower. "Get out of my way, Aidan."

"Fuck you, no. What's your problem?"

His friend narrowed his eyes. "She wants you, asshole."

"No shit. She's ours. It'd be difficult to claim our mate if she didn't want us." He still believed it down to his bones and no matter what anyone said, she belonged to them.

"No, she wants *you*. Not me. *You*." Carson dropped his head back and released a grim laugh. "First time in my life some chick doesn't want me and prefers *you*."

53

The words slammed home, gutting him. "You have a problem with her wanting me? Liking me?" He fought for breath, his lungs still frozen in place. "And you think she likes me over you, and that's what's got you pissed? The idea that a woman we both want, who we crave as a mate, might want me more? That's what you're saying, right? You're enraged because, for once, a female desires me."

He knew without a doubt that Rebecca craved Carson just as much as she yearned for him. She was destined for *them*. Not one or the other.

"They always turn to me, Aidan. Always. And you and her…"

"You don't think she could desire me, do you? I've always been the one females tolerated, and you can't handle the fact that she needs me." Rage, pure molten rage, filled him. His friend, his best friend and fucking Alpha partner… "You've always thought of me as a charity case, haven't you? Poor scarred Aidan, let's always share a woman because then he'd at least get laid."

He shook his head, memories colliding. It was true he'd been self-conscious growing up. Being the bastard son of the Alpha meant rough treatment by the more powerful males. But that wasn't what ruined him. No, that came at the hands of his father's mate.

His father fucked and impregnated Aidan's mother, and then his dad and Alpha partner found their mate. She hadn't appreciated Aidan's presence and tried to end it. Violently and with the help of her family. He'd grown into his scars, accepted them as part of him even though they fucked with his head.

There was a truth, however. Between his size and the wounds, he scared the hell out of people. Women included.

So when he'd met and connected with Carson in his early twenties, he'd still been a virgin.

Carson was the one who said they should always share. They should be experienced in pleasuring their shared mate and what better way to do that than to always take a woman together?

"I was always a pity fuck, wasn't I?" The emotions crushed him, years of partnership crumbling before his eyes. "You got them into bed and convinced them to let me touch them, bring them pleasure." His throat squeezed. "Every one of them closed their eyes when I touched them, and you fucking told me it was okay."

Instead of answering, Carson turned his head away and stared at the far wall. Well, that was answer enough, wasn't it?

Aidan stepped back, disgust overruling every other feeling swirling through him. "Fuck you, Carson." The words were hoarse, and he cursed himself for showing the hurt. "Get the fuck out. I don't give a damn where you go and what you do, but get the fuck out before I kill you."

Carson still wouldn't look at him. "It doesn't have to be this way. She isn't ours. Despite the pull, she doesn't belong to us. She's ruining it and—"

"You may not want her, but I do. If she's not ours, she sure as fuck is *mine*." He swallowed past the lump in his throat. "I'll petition the Ruling Alphas to dissolve our bond."

His partner swung his gaze to Aidan, eyes wide. "You're going to destroy us over a woman?"

Aidan shook his head. "No, you destroyed us long ago. There are no secrets in an Alpha Pair, Carson. Even I know that. But you managed to keep this bottled up, and I refuse to be tied to a male who can't be honest with me, one who's spent years pitying me. I deserve better. Rebecca deserves better." He took a deep breath. "Get out. Stay somewhere else, I don't give a fuck where, but you need to be gone before she gets out of the shower."

Time stood still, two Alphas with their stares locked and neither backing down. It was a pure moment of truth and dominance. One of them would flinch, one of them would end the game and relent. It wouldn't be Aidan. He had too much at stake. Mainly his future with Rebecca. Maybe he had been wrong all those years ago. Maybe he'd felt a pull toward Carson, but it hadn't been the need to form a pair.

Maybe there was a male out there truly meant to finish his triad with Rebecca. Because it sure as hell wasn't Carson. Their future hung in the balance, stretched taut between them, and it was his partner who flinched first.

Carson jerked his attention from Aidan and moved around him, putting distance between them. "I'll send a bellhop for my stuff."

Aidan nodded but didn't say a word. He couldn't.

He listened to Carson's progress, the sound of the man's boots on the polished marble. One step turned into a dozen and then they paused at the door. The jingle of the chair scraping against metal snapped through the quiet.

But Aidan couldn't leave well enough alone. He thought back through their few meetings with Rebecca and only came up with one instance when she shied from their touch.

The knob clicked, disengaging the lock, and Aidan's voice rang through the room. "Did you stop and think that maybe we were overwhelming her?" He turned toward his friend.

56

"Did you think that the two of us surrounding her in the middle of a packed hallway, minutes after being told about werewolves and then she's left with virtual strangers… That might have frightened her? Perhaps she wasn't cringing, but merely stepping back because she needed space, and I happened to be there. We were hot and hard for her, two men she didn't know, and she was frightened. I know you didn't scent a hint of disgust, Carson. I know that aroma, I've smelled it often enough when we fucked the same woman. Rebecca wasn't repulsed by us; she was scared and aroused." Carson frowned but didn't say a word. "But that doesn't matter because this"—he waved a hand between them—"this is fucked."

Carson opened his mouth to speak, but Aidan overrode him. "So you take your pitying ass out of here. I don't want you here."

"What about her? You said…" His friend's voice was hoarse, but it was a soft feminine alto that answered.

"She doesn't want you here either." Rebecca stepped from her room, wrapped in the fluffy robe he'd left for her. Her skin was flushed and damp from her shower, but her stare was icy cold.

"Rebecca…" Carson tried and Aidan recognized his friend's remorse, but the pain was too deep.

Rebecca shook her head. "No. Whatever this is"—she gestured to the three of them—"Aidan's right." She stepped further into the room. Her visible pain had him aching to go to her, to wrap her in his arms. "You've spent years…" She looked to Aidan. "How many years?"

"Fourteen." Aidan pushed the word past his pain.

"For fourteen years you've pitied him. I may not know all there is to know about your kind, but I sure as hell know I wouldn't want to be with someone who stayed out of pity." She fisted the lapels of the robe, hands shaking, and then she lowered them along the seam. She stopped mid-thigh, trembles still wracking her body. "If we worked this out, if somehow..."

God, Aidan wished, hoped, and prayed they could.

Rebecca shuddered. "Would you stay with me out of pity?"

"Rebecca," Carson wheezed. "Wha—?"

She was careful as she parted the fluffy fabric, gentle as she eased one half open to expose a portion of her thigh. Any other time, Aidan would drop to his knees and beg her for a taste, for a chance to savor that pale skin. But now, in the middle of *this* conversation, while they discussed pain and scars and the future... his heart ached for her.

Scars. Burn scars. They crisscrossed her thigh, stopping a few inches above her knee, but he wondered how high they crawled over her body. Did they stop at her stomach, progress to her breasts? He'd admired the slope of the plump mounds, but what had her clothing hidden? He didn't pity this beautiful woman, but he was physically ill when he thought of the pain she endured.

"Would you see this and cringe? Keep me even if you felt sorry for me?"

"It wasn't—" Carson tried again and once again, she shook her head.

"No. Aidan was right when he said I was overcome by all of the information I'd been fed, combined with your presence. And you know what? Maybe I did lean toward him. Maybe I did it because I saw this man who was unashamed by his scars, who walked around like he didn't give a fuck. Maybe it made me think that if a guy like him, one who was gorgeous and confident despite the pain of his past, wanted someone like me... Maybe it meant he wouldn't be disgusted by these scars." She dropped her robe back into place, covering the twisted flesh. "And maybe his Alpha partner might feel that way, too. But"—she shrugged—"you're repulsed, and it is what it is. You're not the first. Hopefully, if we can figure out this weird mating thing—because, god, I want you— we'll find a wolf who doesn't care."

Carson took a step forward and away from the opened door. "Rebecca, wait."

His mate padded toward him, and he lifted his arm for her, welcoming her and holding her close as she cuddled against him. "Right now... It's best if you go."

So Carson did.

And Aidan prayed his own heart would stop hurting someday.

CHAPTER SIX

Rebecca's hands shook. She didn't know why she was so affected by the fight between Aidan and Carson. It was between them. It didn't include her. And yet…

It hit so close to home. It reminded her of the men she'd dated and their reaction to her body, to their attempts at intimacy and the eventual ending of relationships.

Because she'd been burned. Because she'd been hurt as a child and lived with the effects every day. Who were they to be disgusted? They didn't *live* with the stinging sensations when certain types of cloth brushed the scars. They didn't live with the tightness and need to massage the twisted skin even after all these years.

Aidan squeezed her shoulder, his heat sinking through the terrycloth robe. The weight of his lingering kiss on the top of her head soothed her but didn't lessen the trembles and emotions thrumming through her.

Her past had come calling in the form of a man she was attracted to—more than attracted—and she'd answered the door.

"You okay?" he murmured against the top of her head.

No.

"Yeah."

"I'm sorry you had to hear that, see that."

"Better now than later, right? And, you know, the whole Mark thing…" She had to keep reminding herself. Each time she forgot, she let her fantasies take her farther into her imagined future. From kisses, to sex, to early mornings, and child—

"You heard what I said."

Yeah, she was his no matter what. The possessive words should have annoyed her. Instead, they soothed her nerves. "I know."

"You gonna be okay if I go change real quick? I need to speak to Madden and Keller and showing up in ratty jeans and a holey T-shirt won't help my cause."

She pulled back and tilted her head up to meet his gaze. "Do you really want to do this? Break your bond? You're upset now, but he's been with you for so long, Aidan. I worry you'll make a mistake. You'll think things over and…"

And change his mind.

"No, it's the right decision. Trust is a big thing within an Alpha Pair. We have to depend on each other and rule as one. It's broken, and it's best we part ways while we're still young enough to join with another to find happiness." He tucked her wet hair behind her ear. "I can't mate you fully unless we have another Alpha, and Rebecca, I want to claim you more than I want to breathe."

Tears sprung to her eyes, and she fought to blink them back. "Okay." She nodded. "Okay. Go change, and while you talk to them I can sit with my cousins."

"Sounds like a plan." He dropped a kiss to her lips and stepped away. "A concierge should be bringing some clothing for you. My wallet is on the small table near the door. Give him a twenty. If someone comes looking for Carson's stuff, tell him to come back later."

Rebecca rolled her eyes. "How long is it gonna take you to change, five minutes? I doubt someone's gonna show up during that time. And if they do, I'm a big girl."

That earned her a growl from Aidan, and she was in his arms again, his hands spanning her ass. "You are and I love it. All soft curves for me." He squeezed her cheeks and the seductive sensations passed to her pussy, tugging a moan from her chest. He immediately softened his touch and pulled away. "Did I hurt you? I don't know the extent of your scars. You need to tell me if they're sensitive. I have a few burn scars and some—"

She placed her hand over his mouth. "We can talk about that later, but no, I don't have any there. They're mostly on my front. I love that you care, but you need to change."

God, she loved that he cared.

He gave her one last kiss, one last squeeze, and then strode toward a door on the opposite side of the room. There were two in that direction, and she imagined one must have belonged to Carson. She grimaced, thinking of the events of the last few minutes. The day had been a rollercoaster ride, and she was ready for things to even out, to be steady for half a minute before something else blew up.

With werewolves, she didn't think her life would ever be smooth again.

Of course, within thirty seconds of Aidan disappearing, someone knocked on the door.

With a groan, she padded toward the entry to the suite, tightening the belt at her waist while ensuring she was covered. She peeked through the peephole and spotted a male dressed in a hotel uniform waiting in the hallway, clothes swinging from hangers in hand.

Rebecca snatched up Aidan's wallet and flipped it open. Something inside her cringed at going through his belongings. It was weird to dig through the man's wallet. But she did it anyway and plucked out a twenty.

Another knock and she rolled her eyes. Impatient.

She turned the handle and tugged the door open, smiling at the male before her. "Hi, how are you?"

"Miss Twynham?"

"Yes, thanks so much for getting these for me, I really appreciate it." She reached for the hangers with one hand while passing over the cash with the other. Not waiting for a response, she moved to ease the door closed, but the man placed his booted foot against the panel, stopping the movement.

"I have a message for you, as well."

Rebecca frowned and tilted her head to the side. No one knew she was here, and if it was from Carson, she wasn't quite ready for it yet. "Message?"

The man presented a small envelope and Rebecca tucked the clothing beneath her arm as she fought to open the message.

Hi Rebecca,

Come on up when you get tired of dealing with your mates. We can talk about your Mark and stuff.

Mwah!

Rebecca frowned. Her Mark? But she didn't have one and Scarlet knew…

"Would you like to dress? I can take you to see the Ruling Alpha Mate."

Rebecca shot him a suspicious glance with her brow furrowed. "I can find my own—"

"Rebecca?"

Thank goodness. The guy was giving her the willies, and she so didn't want to deal with his weird, smarmy smile any longer.

"Right here. My clothes came, and I got a note from—" She turned toward the sound of Aidan's voice flowing from behind the partially closed bedroom door. Which put her back to the hotel employee.

Yeah, that was a mistake.

An arm wrapped around her neck, pressed tightly against her throat, and cut off her air. She dropped the clothes and wallet to scratch at the forearm holding her captive.

"Stop it, bitch." A blunt instrument pressed against her back. Hard and small, she wasn't sure if the man held a gun or knife to her body, but it didn't matter, did it? Because hair slid under her palms, and she glanced at the man's arm, at the gray fur escaping his pores.

A werewolf. Of course, in a hotel filled with werewolves and run by werewolves, a crazy man would *be* a werewolf.

Nice.

"Don't say a word. Keep your mouth shut and back the fuck up." He dragged her backwards, not giving her a choice in the matter. With his hold crushing her windpipe, she was forced to remain silent. "We're going downstairs and walking through that fucking lobby and you won't say a word." He tightened his grip. "One syllable and I'll have your mates killed. I've got wolves watching them. One." He squeezed tighter, sending pain racing through her body. "Word."

She fought to observe their surroundings. If there were males watching Aidan, then they had to be nearby, right? But the man's grasp kept her immobile and only able to focus on the empty room, the disorderly furniture, and the archway that separated her from Aidan.

They stumbled through the doorway, panel sliding closed as they departed. She struggled against him, scratching and tugging at his arm. But with each flex and twitch of muscle, her body weakened, her air quickly stifled by the stranger's hold.

She prayed Aidan would appear, that he would stride into the hallway and save her. Unfortunately, that didn't happen and they reached the bank of elevators. The moment he pushed a button, doors slid apart.

Now they spun until he was firm against the back of the elevator, and she was before him, staring at the metal—at her own reflection. Panic filled her eyes, fear and anger warring for dominance while adrenaline rushed her veins. Her stomach revolted at his touch, heaved and clenched at the feel of his skin and fur against hers.

Just before the elevator jerked into motion, Aidan called for her, his voice raised and tinged with worry. "Rebecca? Rebecca!"

Then they were going down, descending and flying past floor after floor. They didn't stop, didn't pause at the levels between their suite and the lobby. She prayed they'd halt, that another set of wolves would step in and rescue her.

But they didn't.

"I've got you now, don't I? They said it couldn't be done, but I did it." His rancid breath fanned her cheek, but it was the proof of his arousal that disgusted her most.

"Wh-Who?" she rasped.

"You'd like to know, wouldn't you?" He ran his nose along her neck, breathing deep. Then his wet lips brushed her ear as he dropped his voice to a whisper. "The families. Too many accepted it, but not me, not us." He licked her cheek, tongue sliding over her skin, and she cringed, jerking from the touch. "You taste like them, too. I have you, and I heard there are more. Just wait until we capture those, as well."

"Look, I don't know what you want, but—"

"We won't have any more of *you* mating into our lines. Old bastards fucked up, but we have it right." His voice cracked, his volume rising and falling in a crazed shift.

Why hadn't *someone* gotten on the fucking elevator?

"I don't know anything about anyone. I was hauled here and maybe you have me confused with someone else." She tried again. She didn't think she'd have luck reasoning with a crazy person, but she had to try. "You wrote the note, right? About my Mark? I don't have one. I'm not mating anyone. I'm a chick who got sucked into the wrong black hole thing. Why don't you let me go and then we can forget this ever—"

Rebecca didn't get to finish, not when his hold tightened once again, and a soft ding filled the small space. There, they were on the first floor, and *now* someone would come to her rescue.

"Remember, not one word or your mates die where they stand."

Unfortunately the closest loiterers were too preoccupied with getting into another elevator to worry about two people coming out of this one. God, they needed to work on this oblivious behavior. Really.

"C'mon. Keep your mouth shut, and we're getting out of here. The rest should join us soon and then we'll line you all up in a row and—"

"Rebecca? What the hell—?" A shout, a familiar voice, rose above the chattering crowd. And yeah, she may be mad at the man, but she'd never been so thankful to hear his voice.

Carson.

Crazy guy swung her around, and the thing that had poked her back pressed against her temple. A gun. Perfect. Of course, a werewolf would use a firearm rather than the teeth and claws nature gave him.

"Don't come any closer." The wolf holding her captive snarled, and she spotted Carson, noted his sudden halt.

Immediately her eyes scanned the area looking for someone who might have a weapon aimed at Carson, someone who could harm him from afar. No matter her anger, she didn't want anyone hurt on her behalf, least of all him. Her body still burned for his touch and nothing, not even harsh words, could banish that need.

"What's going on? Why do you have my ma— What are you doing with her?"

Yeah, not the time to ask questions. She didn't see anyone paying attention to Carson, or her. Mr. Crazy had to have been lying.

Her mate needed to attack the stupid wolf already.

"We're not letting another one of them mate into the families. It's not happening. We stopped it then. We're stopping it again." The muzzle of the gun dug into her skin.

Every wolf surrounding them froze as if suddenly realizing a kidnapping was in progress. Dozens of yellow eyes focused on them, fur sprouting and covering faces while others flexed claws. All the while Carson seemed to grow, his shoulders broadening and stretching.

"Release her and I'll let you live." Growls from the crowd followed the statement, but a glare from Carson had the sound ceasing in an instant.

"No, she has to die. Her and the others. It's what will stop all this. We had to wait, but now it's time and we'll have them all and then—"

The male holding her didn't say another word because while Crazy McCrazyton ranted at Carson, someone else crept up behind them. Rebecca was yanked left, the gun leaving her temple, while the assailant was shoved right. Immediately following the rush of movement, a racing blur of brown fur roared past her and right at the man who'd held her captive.

A familiar scent encased her while large, warm arms encircled her waist. Aidan. He must have noticed her missing and raced down the hotel stairs to reach her. He drew her close, hugging her tight and burying his face in her hair. He inhaled and then shuddered, his hold tightening slightly.

Snarls and growls echoed off the walls, pounding her ears with the rising sounds. Rebecca jerked against Aidan's hold, not wanting to get away, but to turn and hunt for the source. He allowed the move, cradling her while letting her watch the macabre play unfold before them.

Two wolves battled in the center of a loose circle the crowd formed. One was much smaller than the other, but the slighter of the two continued to fight despite the lost cause. The larger swiped, catching the other across the snout, slicing into fur down to bone. The bigger did it again, hitting the male's chest, baring his muscles. The small one tried to retaliate, but another strike scraped its side while the fourth hit his flank.

Blood coated the cream-colored marble, soaking the ground and slickening the smooth surface. While the larger of the two remained solid on the wet floor, the other scrambled for purchase.

Rebecca gasped when yet another blow connected, practically gutting the tenacious shifter.

"The male deserves it, Rebecca. He touched you, planned to harm you. We may have our problems, but Carson still believes he's your mate. He has a right to get his vengeance. As your mate, he is entitled to retribution," Aidan whispered in her ear and her heart clenched with the emotions that accompanied his words.

The smaller wolf was her kidnapper.

The massive wolf battling for her was Carson. And they did have problems lingering between them. Even if they'd kicked Carson from their room only moments ago, her body yearned for his and she held her breath as she waited for the fight to end.

The wolves snarled and leapt at one another, drawing more blood with each shift of muscle and fur. One swipe sank into Carson's chest, spilling more of the animal's blood, and he snarled in response. His determination renewed, he attacked his opponent with a scary ferocity.

Snap, swipe, scrape, bite. It continued, Carson going after the male again and again. His focus was on his adversary, the wolf intent on ending the man's life. He fought on and on and… for her. His rage was palpable, his determination easily visible, and each wound brought forward emotions she wanted to bury in the sand.

Because those feelings called for him, urged her to go to him and forget every cross word they'd shared. Her mate fought and she ached to welcome him with open arms. No. She couldn't, not after…

One last swipe ended the encounter, Carson dealing the killing blow that practically beheaded the male.

What should have disgusted her, thrilled her. She didn't like to rejoice in someone's death, but he hadn't spoken about just killing her, but others. Plus, during her "orientation," Scarlet told her werewolves had a violent structure and justice system, but it's what kept the beasts from destroying everything they came across.

Carson nudged the dead body, probably ensuring the man was well and truly deceased, before turning toward her. She read the question in his eyes, noted the hope that lingered nearby and the fear that overshadowed it all.

With hesitation and uncaring of what lay unsettled between them all, she held a shaky hand out for him. While she accepted the violence, she still harbored a hint of unease when it came to the power he wielded, especially in animal form.

Aidan leaned down once again. "He won't hurt you."

Carson closed the distance between them, glaring and baring his teeth at a few men who eased too close.

When he was within touching distance, and despite the blood, she sank a hand into Carson's fur, resolving to banish the tumultuous emotions that floated between them. The man had protected her, and stood by her even when the past threatened to shove them apart.

She stroked his fur, fingers sliding beyond the blood to the skin beneath. "Let's go back to our room. We have things to talk about, and you need to get clean."

Aidan's voice was low when he agreed with her. "Yes, we do. We can leave cleanup for others. Carson, once you've showered, we'll speak with the Ruling Alphas about this."

Carson whoofed, and she assumed that was his agreement. He stepped forward, seeming to wait and see if she remained alongside him. When she kept pace, he continued toward the elevators.

Right, wrong, or indifferent... this was where she belonged.

CHAPTER SEVEN

No one would pull, or push, Rebecca from Carson's side
again. No one. He'd stick to her like glue. The rage at almost
losing her to some psycho burned him and enraged his wolf
further. Even after destroying the male who'd taken his
mate, the fury seared him.

Mate. Mate. Mate. God, he'd fucked up in so many ways, but
he didn't want to let her go, let them both go. He needed to
fix things.

Except, right now, his beast wanted more blood. It wanted
the man's accomplices. The "they" and "them" he'd
muttered about.

They'd taste so good on his tongue, his teeth ripping their
flesh.

The only thing that kept him from hunting down the
bastards was the woman beside him. Rebecca needed his
protection even if Aidan lurked on her other side.

Rebecca's fingers remained buried in the fur on his back,
sinking deep and fisting his strands. The hold, the sting of
her tugs, kept him grounded, focused on herding her toward
the elevator and not tearing into the dead wolf once again.

She reached for the button with a still shaking hand, missing
twice before Aidan reached past her and depressed the metal
disc. Carson leaned against her, offering his wolf's comfort
until he was able to shift, shower, and embrace her with his
human arms. Rebecca returned the press and stroked
between his ears with her free hand. She didn't seem to mind

the blood and gore, but he figured fear could make a person overlook a lot.

Finally, a soft ding announced the elevator's arrival. It wasn't until that moment he realized silence continued to reign behind them. No shuffle of cloth or thump of shoes on marble. Nothing.

He'd shocked them with his ferocity and rapid destruction. Good. Maybe that'd teach others a lesson. They shouldn't touch what belonged to him. He glanced at Aidan, at the fury coating his partner's features. They shouldn't touch what belonged to them.

The low clunk and whoosh of the doors opening cut through the quiet of those gathered in the lobby remaining motionless. When the metal panels fully parted, they were faced with a familiar group of men and women. It didn't matter that the human recognized the occupants. The wolf refused to allow others near Rebecca.

Snarling, he pushed Rebecca aside with his shoulder, shoving her past Aidan until she was tucked into a small corner of the hallway and he was able to block the path of others. He growled low, the noise echoing off the walls and increasing tenfold. They needed to know she was *his*, and he would protect *his* at all costs.

"Carson?" Aidan's shout overrode Rebecca's, but he didn't care. Protect. He needed to protect their mate. Why wasn't Aidan at his side?

One of the males slowly emerged, stride fluid and body relaxed as he stepped out of the elevator and turned toward him.

The wolf weighed the man, his nose drawing in the male's scent and evaluating his innate power. Alpha? Definitely.

74

Stronger than him? His beast paused, inhaling again and searching past the blood to find his opponent's true scent. Yes, stronger than him. But was he a safe male? One who would help him protect Rebecca? Or would he turn on them as well? Was he one of the "them" and "they"?

The Alpha dropped into a squat, putting him eye level with the wolf. "Hey, Carson. Little bit of trouble down here, huh?"

Carson narrowed his eyes and didn't lower his lip. The amiable tone annoyed him for some reason, and the wolf wanted to claw the Alpha's patronizing smile from his lips. As if sensing Carson's thoughts, Rebecca tugged on him, forcing him to ease closer to her. Force? No, it was more like a silent request he answered with his movements. He was a few hundred pounds of massive male. She wouldn't move him unless he allowed it. He realized that he'd allow anything should she ask.

The Alpha looked over his shoulder. "Hey, Madden? You and Berke talk to Aidan. Figure out why one of my wolves decided gutting another wolf seemed like a good idea."

Madden. An Alpha. A Ruling Alpha. Right.

And the one before him was Keller. Strong male.

They were mated to Scarlet, his mate's cousin.

These could be trusted. Trusted to protect and care for Rebecca. Trusted not to hurt her.

Some of his tension eased, his wolf releasing a relieved huff.

"That's it," Keller murmured and extended his hand.

Even though Carson accepted and recognized Keller as his Alpha, he couldn't let down his guard. Others still lurked. He trusted Keller's strength, but Rebecca was his responsibility, his mate. The thought had him curling his lip again, exposing his long fangs in a silent threat.

The Ruling Alpha sighed and dropped his hand. "It's like that?" Keller pushed to his feet. "Fine. Jack, Emmett, and Levy are in the elevator along with our mates. It was a tight fit, lemme tell you, but the women wouldn't be left behind."

One of those women, Scarlet, poked her head out of the elevator, drawing Carson's attention. "Can we come out now? I mean, I can see the Field-o-Death from here. The guy is really, *really* dead."

No, that couldn't happen. The evil male...

Carson fully curled back his lips, exposing all of his teeth, and his rumbling echo caused a charged silence to overtake the area.

Keller tilted his head in question, his gaze never leaving Carson's, but he refused to back down. The females needed to stay safe, should remain with their mates. Joining the increasing crowd was dangerous.

The Ruling Alpha glanced over his shoulder at the Alpha Mate. "That's not a good idea."

"But—"

Carson released a snapping bark and then upped the volume of his growl.

"No, you stay put." Keller's voice left no room for argument and Scarlet disappeared into the elevator. Good. The Ruling Alpha focused on him again. "Okay, we're keeping the mates

away and you look like you want to keep yours safe."
Another ding, another elevator arriving had the male pausing to look toward the new arrivals. Carson recognized them as men from the Ruling Alpha's personal guard. "My men are here. Join the mates in the elevator. I'll grab Madden, Berke, and Aidan. We can all go up and discuss this."

Carson didn't want to move, didn't want to budge an inch. No one could sneak up on him as long as he remained in place. No one could surprise him and take Rebecca again. No one could...

"Carson," Aidan cut into his thoughts. "I know what you're trying to do. Let's get her safe in the Ruling Alpha's suite. They need you both to talk about what happened so they can level judgment. That's the safest place in the hotel."

"Judgment?" Rebecca gasped, and Carson glared at Aidan.

The male held up his hands. "We both know nothing will come of it, but we also know we need to get her out of here. The wolves are getting restless and curious. How long is it before one of them decides they want to figure out what makes her special, Carson?"

Carson pulled his glower from his friend and focused it on the growing group. Yes. Curious was one word to describe the crowd. Lustful and desirous were others.

With a low chuff, he stepped away and gave Rebecca enough space to walk beside him, his body acting as a barrier between her and the gathered werewolves. Aidan took a step toward them, question in his gaze, and Carson didn't object when the male took up a protective stance.

Aidan was one to be trusted with Rebecca. He was her mate, his partner, his friend. The male wouldn't allow harm to come to her, the wolf understood that.

The men and women shuffled in place and Aidan met more than one pair of glowing yellowed eyes. Their wolves were near the surface, the scent drawing forward the beasts of the weaker attendants.

When they reached the opened doors, Carson urged Rebecca into the space. It wasn't long before Madden and Berke returned, murderous glares in place. The rage rolling off them wasn't directed at Carson, so he didn't give a damn about their emotions. He was concerned with getting his mate safe. Not much time passed and the doors swooshed closed. He'd never been more thankful for freight elevators in his life. It allowed some of the most powerful males in all the packs to accompany them to the penthouse.

Protection in droves.

No one said a word as they made their ascent, their travels unimpeded by stops at other floors. He imagined the Ruling Alphas were able to override certain functions. That seemed to include bypassing all floors and allowing them to rise uninterrupted.

It didn't take long for the elevator to ding. The doors spread once again and the riders spilled into the entryway.

Keller took control right away. "Living room. Carson, the spare room is to the left. Shift and shower. I won't have my rooms smelling like wet wolf and blood."

He would have snorted had he a human nose. Instead, he merely grabbed a portion of Rebecca's robe with his teeth and led her toward the open doorway. He didn't have a claim to her, but he couldn't let her out of his sight. He just… needed her close.

He was halted by Keller's next words. "I need her here. She needs to give testimony."

78

Fuck that. He didn't hesitate to voice his objections, wolf releasing an audible threat.

When Madden stepped forward, Scarlet intervened. "Hey, if it were me, you wouldn't let me out of your sight, would you?" She glared at Keller and then directed her anger at Madden. "And if I remember correctly, you *didn't* last year when that wolf brought me food and you snarled and growled."

Both men turned their frustration on their mate for a moment, and then Madden focused on him and Rebecca. "Fine. Make it quick."

That had Carson going back into action, tugging his mate along. He sensed Aidan following them, hot on their heels.

He whoofed in response. Yes, they could both care for her.

Turning from Aidan, he resumed their trek, padding through the spare room and straight into the bathroom. He dropped Rebecca's robe as he passed through the doorway only to hear her take another two steps toward him.

He halted and turned back to her, his aches finally making themselves known. He pushed them back as he waited to find out what caused Rebecca to follow him.

"Are you—" She cleared her throat and a tremble wracked her. "Are you okay?"

The scents of her worry and heartbreak reached him and he realized they'd never get anywhere unless he was on two feet. A few of the cuts and scrapes he'd acquired still burned and ached. They wouldn't heal quickly without a shift, so he pushed his animal to the back of his mind and beckoned his human half forward. The wolf readily agreed, accepting his logic and desperate to soothe their mate.

His skin stretched, bones snapped and reformed while muscles lengthened and shortened as needed. It took no time to go from battered wolf to slightly less battered human.

Rebecca gasped, eyes widening, and she took a step back as she pressed a hand to her chest. In fear of him? His heart squeezed, and he fought to remind himself werewolves were new to her. She wasn't familiar with shifts; men and women changing to wolves and back again.

Instead of reaching for her, Carson remained in place. "It's okay. I'm not going to hurt you."

Eventually, she found her voice. "Hurt me? I know you won't hurt me." She shook her head. "There's so much blood. Oh god, Carson, there's so much."

So she wasn't scared of him. He hadn't realized the worry that weighed on him, but suddenly his shoulders felt lighter with her words.

"Carson?" Aidan called to him, and he turned his attention to his friend, noting the worry coating his features.

He tore his gaze from the man and refocused on Rebecca. Her concern was palpable and reached into his soul. "I'm fine." He gestured to his body, encompassing himself with a sweep from head to toe. "Most of this is his."

Still, tears entered her eyes, gathering on her lashes and then trailing down her cheeks.

He reached for her, extending his arm and holding his palm flat. "I'm fine."

She rushed to him, carefully wrapping her arms around his middle, and he returned the embrace. He'd almost lost her before he had her. Had he been a moment too late... It wasn't worth worrying about. He had her with him, safe and sound and at his side.

Carson leaned down to press a kiss to Rebecca's head, risking her rejection while hoping to reassure her. Her body trembled, sniffles and sobs escaping her lips. "Shh... I'm fine."

"I-I-I was so scared and he... and you... You can't do that, Carson. I can't... I don't know how or why I feel like this, even after... but you can't do that to me."

"I'm okay. It's the way wolves are." He laid his cheek atop her head. "We're bloody and violent, but I promise I'll never hurt you and I'll keep others from getting near you. I promise. What happened downstairs—never again."

Another wave of shakes overtook her, and he held her throughout, waiting for the sharp edge of fear to release her. It was wrong of him, but he reveled in the opportunity to touch her. Jealousy had nearly cost him everything and he resolved to push the emotions aside. Pride was nothing when compared to having his mate in his arms.

It took time, minutes ticking past as they clutched each other while Aidan looked on. The man's gaze was a heavy weight on Carson's shoulders, but he couldn't spare a glance for the male, and he was sure his friend's expression wasn't one of welcome. His entire focus needed to remain on his mate.

Eventually, the shudders lessened, and she relaxed against him with a sigh.

"You okay?"

"No." She shook her head, and he smiled.

"You will be. I need to wash and so do you." While he'd enjoyed their hug, the dead wolf's blood now coated her robe. "Let Aidan comfort you and I'll see you both in the living room."

Even as the pain from losing her touch speared him, Carson was heartened by her reluctance to leave his embrace, at the way her feet shuffled across the tile and rugs decorating the floor. She was just as unwilling to leave him as he was uneasy with her easing from his protection.

Now he needed to convince her, and Aidan, that despite the pain he'd caused, they should never let him go.

CHAPTER EIGHT

Carson knew he didn't have the right to touch or hold Rebecca close and assure himself she was fine. More than fine. She was uninjured and hadn't suffered more than a bruise from her ordeal.

That didn't soothe his wolf. No, it enraged the beast. The animal was furious at the wolf who'd threatened her and focused even more of its fury on Carson's human half.

The beast couldn't inflict any more pain than he leveled on himself.

Watching Rebecca and Aidan leave the bathroom hand in hand as he remained in place, covered in blood and gore, was one of the hardest things he'd ever done. The wolf needed her with him. He'd fought to save her and now he wanted her within sight. The ache was second only to allowing Aidan to thrust Carson from his life. His heart knew the truth, knew he was born to rule at Aidan's side. But his mind only saw the twenty-year-old Alpha who was afraid to approach a woman. His friend could face down the most fearsome opponent without a blink, but a female was another story.

At least, it had been *then*.

After the first time, the tradition was carried forward through the years, Carson choosing a female, convincing them of Aidan's worth and the pleasure they'd receive, followed by an explosive encounter that lasted hour after hour.

And somewhere along the way, he'd fucked it all up. Now, seeing them together, he realized everything he'd lost.

Years of habits had cost him his future.

Because Rebecca *was* theirs. His *and* Aidan's. He didn't give a fuck what tradition said. Rebecca belonged to them both. He'd find a way to apologize, to work his way back into their lives, and then they'd claim the woman as their own. He hoped he did it soon, before too much time passed and he was left with nothing.

Standing in the middle of the Ruling Alphas' suite and waiting for Rebecca and Aidan, he was anxious to repair the damage he'd caused. He just needed one chance, a handful of moments to plead his case.

Eventually Aidan and Rebecca, in a new robe and clean of blood from her hug with Carson, emerged from one of the other rooms within the suite, the scent of arousal and hints of desire clinging to them. The only thing that saved his sanity was the fact he didn't think they'd made love as Carson sat battling his wolf's need for her.

They held hands as they emerged, faces flushed but no less worried.

A low snicker came from across the room. "Had a good time, didn't you?"

The man was obviously an idiot. Desire and sex held two distinct scents.

Rebecca blushed, and Aidan growled, but Carson went into action. He zeroed in on the offending man, moving from one side of the room to the other in a blink. He wrapped his claw-tipped fingers around the male's throat before he could utter a sound.

Carson squeezed and lifted the wolf until his feet dangled. "Do you have something to say?"

Red-faced and gasping, the wolf pushed out a single word. "No."

Carson leaned close, grip remaining firm. "I didn't hear you. Do you have something to say? I'm thinking it should sound like an apology to my mate."

He internally winced at the slip, but refused to stutter and stammer over the words.

"I-I-I'm s-s-s-sorry."

"And you're never going to do it again, are you?" He kept his tone even and calm. He couldn't allow his wolf to tear away any more control because then he'd be ripping the male to shreds.

"No. Never."

An annoyed sigh reached him and was immediately followed by Keller's irritated voice. "Carson, can you please put the idiot Warden down? We need him for a little while. You can kill him later."

"How much later?" Carson's wolf was intrigued by the idea of a time limit. That meant he would eventually get a piece of the Warden.

"A few days."

"Ten minutes. Fifteen tops." Madden's voice overrode Keller's lie. The gentler—yet deadly—Ruling Alpha was too easy on the idiots.

With a final, threatening snarl, he released the wolf and stepped back as the male fell to the ground in a gasping pile. Giving the Warden one last glare, he strode back across the room and took up a post behind the couch where Aidan and Rebecca now sat.

Rebecca shot him an incredulous look, mouth and eyes wide open, while Aidan's was dark and calculating. He knew his words stunned the duo, but now wasn't the time to plead his case. He hoped it would be soon, though.

The still red-faced Warden joined the small group. Several loveseats were turned in a loose circle, each occupied by one of the Wickham sisters and their mates. The last held the idiot werewolf and who Carson assumed was his Warden partner.

"Okay." Keller clapped his hands. "Let's get started. First, I want to discuss the dead wolf in the lobby and Rebecca's brief kidnapping."

Carson gripped his own biceps, fighting the urge to wrap his arms around Rebecca. Staring at the back of her head, at the way she leaned against his partner and sought comfort from him, speared Carson's heart. It could have been him with them on the loveseat had he not destroyed their partnership. But they were still tied together despite Aidan's earlier words. Only the most powerful Warden Pair could sever the bond.

He wouldn't say a word to the Ruling Wardens, Emmett and Levy. He hoped Aidan would keep his mouth shut as well.

"Rebecca, you start." Keller's order had Rebecca snuggling deeper into Aidan's hold while the other males in the room leaned slightly forward.

Carson eased even closer until his thighs brushed the back of the couch and he leveled a glare on them all. They could listen, but he didn't want any of them frightening her. He'd done that enough on his own.

He didn't relax as Rebecca told her story. If anything, he tensed further as thoughts of the recent past took over. The male's words had been crazed and rambling, spouting nonsense as he'd held a gun to his mate. The threat on Rebecca's life still had him on edge, but even more so, on the men and women littered through the space.

Emmett was the first to speak. "He said families? Plural?"

Rebecca nodded. "Yes. Does that mean anything? I didn't understand."

Levy ran a hand through his hair. "Yeah, yeah, it does."

Whitney, their Warden Born mate, glowed, her skin brightening as the multitude of marks covering her shone. That was what happened when a Warden Born female found her Warden mates. They formed a powerful, almost invincible triad of wolven strength and magic.

He recalled the summary he and Aidan received shortly after last year's Gathering. Emmett and Levy discovered that contrary to werewolf laws and popular belief, Wardens *could* have a mate, and their coming together would strengthen their powers.

The only reason no one remembered was due to magical manipulation of the summoning spell by the leaders of the five families.

Oh, god.

"It's the families, the five families, isn't it?" His voice was hoarse with emotion, strangled by the implications. "Whitney's a Wickham and you pissed them off and now they're after…"

A low, rumbling growl from Emmett reached him, but he didn't give a damn. Crazed members of the five oldest, most powerful werewolf families had gone after Rebecca. His Rebecca.

"Enough." Madden's snap shot through the room, silencing them all.

"Yes." Keller's answer filled the quiet. "We spoke to the new patriarch of each after the last Gathering and every male assured us there would be no reprisal. They understood why Emmett, Levy, and Whitney killed the attacking males. They deserved what they got. Then we offered any help they needed. The actions of the fathers were not endorsed by the sons. Plus, the families haven't caused any trouble since the last Gathering. It seems someone lied, or not everyone agrees with the current leadership and they're picking up the ex-Elders' torch."

"Either option means trouble," Levy murmured and everyone nodded. "But I'm leaning toward a rogue group. Young, incompetent, and stupid—obviously—but still deadly."

"I agree," Madden spoke up. "An adolescent pup could have done a better job." Madden shook his head and sighed. "The *them* mating into our lines has me worried there's a threat to all females, but I think it focuses on Wickham relatives directly. Whitney was part of ending the families. Plus he mentioned the *old bastards*. That could only mean Sarvis and his associates."

Everyone knew of Sarvis. He'd been Emmett and Levy's mentor as well as an Elder. At least until he attempted to end Whitney's life with the help of the other families and ended up dead himself.

"So, we know the threat and that they think there are more Wickhams or Twynhams running around the Gathering." Keller's gaze scanned the room. "We need to find them and protect them while we hunt the men involved in this mess."

Rebecca's voice was subdued when she spoke up. "How?"

"That's why Miles and Holden are here." Emmett gestured toward the two Wardens.

Carson curled his lip at the still red-faced male and that earned him a glare from the Ruling Warden. He didn't care. The man's presence still pissed him off.

Emmett continued. "They have a few specialties, but the one we're concerned with is their ability to find others, human, wolf, it doesn't matter. Which means we can use that gift to find those in the Twynham line and discover if they've been hauled to the Gathering. They've already confirmed there aren't any Wickhams in the hotel."

Carson unfolded his arms and gripped the back of the couch, not liking how the two males stared at Rebecca. Could they still do their jobs if they were blinded? He was more than willing to test the theory.

Levy cleared his throat and narrowed his eyes at Carson. "They can also determine if a female is destined to mate with a pair of wolves."

Carson's body froze, blood no longer pumping through his veins. If a woman was summoned to the Gathering, she was either Alpha Marked or Warden Born. Period. Sure, there'd

89

been some question about Whitney's presence last year, but once the Warden Born were rediscovered, her attendance was explained.

But what about Rebecca?

His mate must have felt the same because she whimpered and buried her face against Aidan's neck. At the same time her small, trembling hand found Carson's, and he grasped her fingers. He didn't want to read too much into her reach for him, but he savored the shaky touch.

"I don't want to know." Rebecca's words were muffled, but based on the frowns everyone wore, they heard.

"Rebecca," Scarlet murmured and climbed from her mates' laps. She padded across the room, and Carson's wolf went on alert. The Ruling Alpha Mate was Rebecca's cousin and yet... "I talked to my mother. It's important you let them do this. I think—she thinks—your accident wasn't an accident."

Carson's heartbeat pounded in his ears, and he heard Rebecca's heart race.

"What do you mean?" his mate rasped.

"Our grandmothers were Marked. Mine ended up in a happy mating while yours didn't." Scarlet's words were soothing and calm. "Mom thinks that maybe you had a Mark and then... at the annual reunion..."

"I was burned. You don't think..."

Carson's heart ached for her, thrummed in empathetic grief.

"I do. Mom's looking for old pictures from before that reunion, before... Maybe she can find something, but these guys can tell for sure right now." Scarlet's gaze met his and

90

he found nothing but sympathy in her eyes. "You'll know if Carson and Aidan are yours once and for all."

Joy suffused him right alongside agony. He'd know she was theirs just as he lost what tied them together.

"Mine." Aidan snarled. "No matter what, she's mine."

The same word burst to his lips, and he swallowed it. He had no right to make a claim. But then Rebecca turned her head and met his eyes. Hers overflowed with tears, pain, and longing. He couldn't have remained still had he tried. Instead, he reached out and cupped her cheek, catching the moisture with his thumb. The tears were like a stab to his heart, the agony rising with each breath until he mouthed the word filling his mind.

"Mine."

Rebecca nodded and turned back to the crouching Scarlet. "Okay."

"Okay." Scarlet grinned. "It's kinda neat, but boring. You stand there, and they stare at you a lot."

The Ruling Alpha Mate rolled her eyes and then stepped aside. When Rebecca rose, Aidan at her side, Carson was quick to round the loveseat and stand at her left. That earned him a glare from Aidan, but Rebecca clutched his hand.

He'd take her affection over Aidan's anger any day of the week.

Then it was as Scarlet described. Miles and Holden approached, and while Holden glared at him, Miles looked wary. Good, they should both fear him.

"Okay, just relax," the idiot Warden murmured and then there was a lot of standing and staring before they both turned and stared at each other.

That lasted for a second or two and Carson imagined the two males were speaking telepathically before they became intent on their trio once again.

Holden stared at Miles and the man shook his head. "Hell no, I'm not doing it, you do it."

"Damn it, you just have to point," Holden growled.

"I'm not pointing. You point." Miles was still shaking his head.

"Miles."

"Holden. You were not the one being choked."

Holden dropped his head back to stare at the ceiling. "If you weren't such an ass, that wouldn't have happened."

Miles shrugged. "I am who I am."

Carson would have been happier if the man at least apologized for being a dick. Instead of waiting for them to see who'd grow a set of balls first, he growled. "Just say it already."

Miles glared and stepped closer, extending his hand and pointing at Rebecca's right hip. Her skin glowed under the fabric, pulsing with the golden light. "Her Mark is there. We can feel it just beneath the skin. Someone tried to get rid of it."

Carson realized someone had tried to *burn* it from his mate's skin, and that had his blood boiling while his wolf pushed gray fur from his pores. His rolling growl rose in volume and encompassed the space. Someone hurt her in order to hide her from them. Before this moment, she'd felt like theirs, but knowing she was one of the Marked solidified the draw they both sensed.

Miles took a hasty step back. "Someone tried to get rid of it, but it's not something you can remove. The Mark is merely a physical sign that identifies a woman meant for Alphas."

Rebecca trembled and leaned into Aidan, but Carson wouldn't let her pull away from him. Instead, he eased closer and rested his front against her side. She needed to know he was there, too. No matter how much he'd fucked things up, they belonged together. It'd take time for him to prove it to them both.

"You can do that with anyone? Warden Born and Marked?" Rebecca's words were low, but he picked them up thanks to his wolf.

"Yes," Miles nodded.

The move was echoed by Holden. "We can determine if they're destined for a wolf. Warden Born are trickier since we have to fool the magic into thinking we're meant for her instead of her true pair, but it's possible."

Rebecca drew in a ragged breath and released on a hiccupping sob. "I wasn't the only one in that fire. I wasn't the only one hurt. We were in a treehouse when it happened and… I don't think they were meant to be caught in it, but… The three of us… Grandma Twynham had this homemade sunscreen she used on me right there. It burned so hot… That's what did it. It was almost like it called to the fire. But she didn't put it on them. Maybe that means they don't have a mark. They were just caught…"

Her words penetrated his mind, and his heart shattered for her, for her family. Ignoring the tension that lived between the three of them, he wrapped himself around Rebecca while anchoring himself to Aidan with one hand.

Nothing penetrated her cries, her clutching hands, and emotional trembles.

"Who, Rebecca?" Scarlet whispered.

His mate sniffled, and her pain wrapped around him in a viselike grip.

"My sisters, Lorelei and Paisley. They're older than me by a couple of years." Rebecca shuddered. "If they haven't been brought here in the past, then they aren't Marked. Maybe…"

Holden's shaking head followed Rebecca's trailing voice. "It doesn't mean anything. Not if they're Warden Born. Any female who is single, Warden Born, and thirty or older was summoned to the Gathering." His words softened. "It doesn't mean they're here, but they might be, and we'll do our best to find them."

Miles took a tentative step forward. "We need a drop of Rebecca's blood and then—"

Carson caught Rebecca as Aidan shoved her into his arms so he could launch himself at the Warden. Carson was tempted to stop his partner, but when the man's actions meant he got to hold his mate, he figured he'd wait a minute or two.

CHAPTER NINE

Their new suite looked exactly like the previous one with one exception: there were two bedrooms instead of three. Two when there were three people, which meant at least two of them would have to share one space.

Because, after all was said and done in the Ruling Alpha suite, Rebecca, Aidan, and Carson retreated to their accommodations one floor beneath the powerful rulers. It was restricted access, and they now had two guards outside their door at all times. Until the threat was eliminated, the duo would be their constant shadows.

The question now was whether security shadowed a werewolf and a human, or two werewolves and their mate. At the moment, it seemed like a combination since Carson followed them.

Rebecca wasn't sure if she was prepared to face any further drama, and Aidan seemed to know because he suddenly swung her into his arms and strode toward the bedroom on the right. The double doors were spread wide, revealing a tastefully appointed bedroom decorated in deep soothing colors. But what most appealed to her was the massive bed that occupied the center.

Sleep. Sleep would be so awesome.

Aidan strode to the side of the bed and carefully lowered her legs to the floor, her side pressed against his front and her thigh brushing the hard ridge of his cock. She shuddered and slumped against him. The pink bits of her were willing, but she was simply too exhausted to do anything.

Aidan shushed her and simply tugged at her robe, untying the belt and nudging it to pool at her feet. Then he pulled aside the blankets and sheets covering the bed. "In you go."

"I'm naked." She wasn't sure if she cared, but it seemed like she should. Weren't women supposed to be all timid and unsure and shy?

"I know. Get in anyway," he murmured.

She glanced at the welcoming mattress and figured, *fuck it*, and crawled onto the surface. The coolness welcomed her and the moment she settled, he dropped the comforter into place.

Aidan leaned across the bed and swept a soft kiss across her lips. He brushed aside her hair, fingertips stroking her face as he stared into her eyes. It was a searching glance, one that silently asked her if she was okay. Just as quietly, she petted him in return, feeling the rough scruff of his growing beard.

She was fine. Well, fine-ish. It wasn't every day a girl found out her family purposefully gave her the scars that had shaped and formed her life. They'd made her who she was today. Strong. Fierce. Timid. Self-conscious. What would she have been had they not tried to destroy her destiny?

Destiny... One that involved two males. Aidan and— She didn't want to go there. Yes, she was destroyed by the man's behavior, but the emotions were more an extension of Aidan's feelings than entirely her own. She let her attention flick to the doorway, to the dejected male hovering outside the bedroom. He appeared as exhausted as she was, but his seemed to go beyond the physical and even emotional. His soul hurt and beckoned to hers. She wanted to react to his unspoken call.

He belonged to her just as much as Aidan.

Aidan turned his head and followed her line of sight before returning his attention to her once again. He eased forward and pressed a gentle kiss to her forehead. "Give me a second and I'll come to bed."

Rebecca nodded. Maybe the two men would talk and settle things between them. Aidan would either return with Carson or come back alone. She wasn't sure which she preferred.

Who was she kidding? She wanted them to reappear together. He was her other Alpha, and she wanted him at her side, protecting and loving her.

When Aidan moved as if to rise, she grabbed his forearm.

"I want what you want, Aidan." She pulled in a breath and released it slowly. "If that's..."

"Hush. You need sleep."

She tried again. "But I want you to know that—"

He quieted her with a quick kiss. "I know what you mean and your acceptance makes me want to crawl into this bed with you and make love to you until the sun rises. But we can't. So you need to sleep, and I need to settle things with Carson."

"Okay," she sighed. "But you'll come back soon?" She raised her eyebrows, hopeful he'd tell her yes.

"Of course. I can't stay away from you for long, not now that I know you're mine." His seductive grin gave her body ideas, but instead of exploring them, he stepped away. "Sleep."

Rebecca glanced at Carson, still hanging around the doorway. She looked at him and noted the hope and need in his gaze. Yes, she hoped the two men worked things out between them so they could begin their mated lives.

Her attention was snared by Aidan as he paced through the room, first ducking his head down to look under the bed and striding toward other doors. He pulled them aside to check behind them and then he entered the bathroom. It wasn't long before he reappeared.

"Thank you." She gave him a small smile.

"For what?" Aidan raised his eyebrows high.

"For making sure I'm safe."

His eyes softened, sweet and gentle emotions filling his gaze. "I'll always fight to keep you safe, Rebecca. You're the most important thing in my world, and I refuse to lose you again."

The rustle of clothing drew their attention to Carson and his expression told her he felt the same.

They were so different, yet very much the same. Their intentions were good. Their hearts were in the right place, and it was only her appearance that had derailed their partnership. She hoped it hadn't permanently ended it.

Maybe it was the urge to mate the men or the fact they both looked at her like she was a juicy steak—which said a lot since they were wolves—but she wanted them to work out their difficulties and come to her.

Aidan strode to the bedroom doors and snagged the handle of one, tugging it closed behind him. He reached for the other, giving it the same treatment. The last thing she saw was the grim expression on Aidan's face and the restrained hope on Carson's.

*

Aidan paused a moment and stared at the closed double doors. His mate—*his mate*—lay beyond the wood panels, safe and sound in the comfortable bed. He wished he was there, cuddled against her and breathing in her sweet scent. Movement to his left reminded him why he wasn't currently wrapping Rebecca in his arms.

"Let's sit." Aidan turned from the bedroom door and strode to the sitting area that occupied the space between the two rooms. He dropped into one of the plush chairs, letting the seat welcome him, and he allowed some of the tensions of the day to drain away.

Carson eased on the seat opposite him, gingerly lowering himself to perch on the edge. The man tried to hide his nervousness but after fourteen years, Aidan saw past the attempt. There were no secrets between the two of them and they'd long ago learned to read one another.

No secrets… There was one, wasn't there? One that stretched their entire relationship.

Relationship. He sounded like a fucking girl.

Well, he wasn't going to act like one.

"What do you want, Carson?"

His friend—ex-friend?—released a mirthless laugh. "God, what *don't* I want?" Carson shook his head. "I fucked up. There. I fucked up fourteen years ago, and I've been fucking up ever since, but it's…" He breathed deep and met Aidan's gaze. "It wasn't like that."

Aidan snorted. "It was exactly like that." He leaned forward, placing elbows on his knees. "Was I a pity partner? Did you see the poor kid without a family? The boy whose stepmother tore him to shreds with nothing but her claws?"

"*It wasn't like that.*"

He rolled his eyes, deflecting instead of thinking about his past. It wasn't pretty, it was downright fugly, and he didn't want to go there. "*It was exactly like that.* I don't need anyone's pity. I didn't need it then. I don't need it now."

"Aidan…"

Aidan pushed to his feet. "I don't need to hear anymore."

Carson mirrored him but while Aidan adopted an uncaring attitude, the male was angrier than Aidan had ever seen. "Sit the fuck down, asshole."

"Fuck you, I don't need this." Trying to go there had been a mistake.

"Yeah, you fucking do. Because fourteen years ago I didn't see a fucking kid whose mother was a raging cunt. I saw a man who'd fucking *survived.* He took all of her shit. He'd been captured by his stepmother's brother and the two of them carved his skin with their nails."

Aidan didn't want a recap. The memories, nightmares, still plagued him all these years later. "I don't need the highlight reel."

"Listen. For once, just listen." His friend stared at him with begging eyes, and Aidan kept his mouth shut when Carson continued. "Then, when he got free, he managed to restrain himself. He didn't let his rage overtake him when he was no longer tied to that table. Yes, he slaughtered the male, but he restrained himself with her."

Aidan shrugged and refused to examine why he'd let her live. He had the right. By the law, he could have slit her throat as easily as he had the male's. Emotion, their history, stayed his hand.

"Instead, he healed and called the Territory Alpha to haul her ass in. He led that pack until I found him, and we became one of the most powerful Alpha Pairs in the fucking Midwest." Carson deflated a little, his chest heaving after roaring those words. "And it's not because of me, Aidan. It's you. I'm along for the ride. I attached myself to you out of some misplaced belief I could help you, that someone like you needed me, but—" Carson shook his head. "It's the other way around. It has been for more years than I want to think about."

Aidan furrowed his brow. "What are you saying?"

"I'm saying"—Carson slumped onto the couch—"I'm saying that fourteen years ago I was a douche and an asshole, but I haven't been *that* douche and *that* asshole for a long time."

Aidan retook his seat, but remained perched on the edge and a hint of hope reentered his gaze.

"I'm a dick, Aidan. You know that. And back then, I did see myself as your savior. I was older and 'wiser' and thought I knew better. Yeah, I may have gotten you laid the first few times, but after that…" Carson sighed. "Then women wanted both of us. Sure, sometimes your scars are hard to look at."

Aidan's wolf bristled at his friend's words. They were earned in battle, damn it. It'd been a fight for his life, and he'd survived.

"I mean, you see them and all you can think is *pain*. Like, holy fuck *pain*. And yeah, I was pissed she shied away from me. I know you want to look scary as fuck to people. It's what you do because you're all emotionally fucked—"

"Fuck you." Aidan's words didn't have any heat. He couldn't exactly get too pissed when he *knew* he was emotionally fucked.

"You push everyone away. Except her. She clung to you, and I thought she pulled away from me, and I love you, man, but you're not pretty like me. You're rough, and you don't give a shit what people say. I'm the smooth talker, and you wanna bend a girl over and fuck her 'til she screams. It pissed me off and then—" Carson waved a hand. "It all got fucked up."

Yeah, it did. Fucked up beyond all recognition. *FUBAR.*

Aidan pushed to his feet once again and stared down at Carson, his friend and his partner. The man looked so damned beaten and emotionally bruised. Fuck, now the guy had him sounding all sweet and shit.

"You done?"

"Yeah." Carson slumped further. "Does 'I'm sorry' help?"

"I dunno." Aidan shrugged. "You done acting like a big vagina?"

A low click preceded the opening of their bedroom door, panel swinging wide to expose a sheet-clad Rebecca.

"Sweetheart?" Aidan stepped toward her, avoiding the coffee table and loveseat.

"You were yelling," she murmured, her attention leaving him—probably landing on Carson—and then returned.

"Yeah, well, your mates tend to do that," he murmured and tugged her close. She smelled so damned sweet and clean and purely his. No, he let his gaze go to Carson. Theirs. "You'll get used to it."

Rebecca stiffened in his embrace, and he rubbed her back, trying to soothe the sudden tension. "Mates? With an 's'? As in plural?"

If Carson got any more hopeful, he'd burst, and Aidan didn't leave the man in suspense. "Yeah, plural. If you can forgive him for being an idiot."

She stroked his chest, drawing his attention from the other man. "The better question is whether you can."

"Yeah. I guess I better. The wolf got pissed at the idea of anyone but him inside you. We're stuck with him."

That had Carson glaring at Aidan. "Your wolf is smarter than you."

"Can't be too smart if he doesn't realize you're a walking, talking pussy." Aidan shrugged.

Rebecca elbowed Aidan.

Aidan grunted.

Carson laughed.

Asshole.

"C'mon. I'm tired. I wanna crawl in bed with my mate and never leave." Aidan nudged and prodded Rebecca until she shuffled into the bedroom once again. When he didn't hear any heavy footsteps behind him, he turned back to Carson. "You coming?"

"Uh…" Carson looked from him to Rebecca's retreating form and back again.

Aidan rolled his eyes. "C'mon. I swear if I didn't know you had a dick, I would think you really do have a vagina."

He spun on his heel and went into the bedroom, kicking off his shoes and stripping as he went. And if he smiled, it wasn't because his friend was joining him. Nah, it was because he was crawling into bed with the most beautiful woman in the world.

The one he'd share with Carson.

If the guy would grow some balls already.

It didn't take long for the man to grow them because suddenly the male was there, crawling into bed on Rebecca's right side while Aidan took her left. When he spotted Carson's boxers still hanging on the man's hips, Aidan raised an eyebrow in question.

Carson shrugged. "Didn't wanna assume. You two are letting me into your lives. Don't wanna fuck it up."

Carson might be worried about modesty, but Aidan wasn't. Naked as the day he was born, he crawled into bed beside his mate—*their mate*—and wiggled close until they were skin to skin.

He shared a small smile with Rebecca, noting her light blush, and he couldn't help but drop a lingering, seductive kiss to her lips.

Rebecca hummed and wiggled closer while looking over her shoulder at Carson and back to Aidan. "Not that tired."

He rolled his eyes. "Yes, that tired. Go to sleep. We can think about more in the morning." He softened his words with a gentle glide of his finger across her cheek. "Wanna hold you all night. The rest can come later."

Rebecca snorted and let her eyes drift close. "You said come."

CHAPTER TEN

Rebecca woke to pure pleasure. Warm breath teased her skin, the breeze quickly followed by the delicious slide of a tongue over her flesh. The hair brushing her hip was long and soft, and she knew it'd be silky to the touch. Aidan looked scary as hell but had the prettiest hair. Those talented lips of his suckled her hotspot, her destroyed Mark heating and calling to her mate. Like a beacon in the night, it begged for attention.

If Aidan was tormenting her, then the hard body pressed against her side was Carson. His heat sank into her body, warming her and teasing her with his muscular frame. He touched her, yet didn't. They were skin-to-skin, but he kept his hands to himself. She imagined he was hard and wanting, but she wasn't sure since his cock was nowhere near her side.

There, but not.

Rebecca slid her hand down her abdomen, fingers ghosting over mangled flesh until she stroked Aidan's skull.

"There she is," he murmured against her flesh.

She hummed in response and rocked her hips, enjoying the sensations of his mouth. He left her Mark and drifted across her stomach, kissing and caressing parts of her until he came to her very center. She spread her legs wider, her thigh nudging Carson's as she opened herself.

Carson whimpered, an honest-to-god whimper from the big, bad male to her right.

She opened her eyes, lashes fluttering and orbs fighting to focus in the darkness. The moment she could see, she met Carson's gaze, saw the need and desire he carried.

He remained restrained, not moving as he watched. His muscles were taut and stretching his skin, bulging with the need to touch. She glanced down his body, noting the rapid rise and fall of his chest and the curves and dips of his trim form. And the cock straining against his boxers. She'd been relieved when he'd crawled into bed with those shorts. Then again, she'd been naked—her heart obviously overpowering good sense—so her desire for clothing was a bit weird.

Now, minutes—hours?—later, she wanted them gone. Especially when Aidan suckled her clit and teased her center with his fingers. She moaned and arched, rocking her hips against his mouth. He sucked hard on the bundle of nerves, almost to the point of pain, and then released her with a low pop. With the freedom came a battering wave of pleasure.

Her eyes wanted to flutter shut, to tear her attention from Carson so she could sink into the sensations without distraction. But she didn't. No, she remained intent on the tense male, let him see her ecstasy.

"Like that, don't you." Aidan's low chuckle sent warm gusts of air across her flesh. "Doesn't she, Carson?"

Carson's eyes flashed yellow, his wolf lurking near, and his voice was a rough growl when he spoke. "She does." His attention skated down her body, his eyes seeming to stroke her with invisible hands. "She loves it."

"She'd enjoy it more with another set of lips, of hands." Aidan scraped his fangs over her inner thigh, and she whined. "Teeth. She likes a wolf's bite." Aidan sucked on her flesh, nibbling near her pussy but not quite close enough. "Give her pleasure, Carson."

Rebecca froze, Carson right along with her, and she looked down her body to focus on Aidan. "Aidan? He…"

"Is an idiot, but he's our idiot." Aidan rose from his place between her thighs and crawled until he hovered above her, his hips snug against hers. She gasped when the whole, heated length of him settled along the lips of her pussy and moaned when he slid his hardness over her.

He captured her lips in a lazy, drugging kiss. His lips tasted of her, his tongue still harboring hints of her flavors, and she drew them in. He'd loved on her, given her pleasure, and now the eroticism of kissing him immediately after stoked her arousal. The gentle meeting of mouths ended and Aidan encouraged her to turn her head, to stare at Carson.

"Look at him. He wants you so badly. He's an idiot. He knows he fucked up. We made our peace. The question is, do you want him, Rebecca? Can you forgive him so we can both take you and claim you?"

There was so much hope and longing in his gaze it nearly crushed her with its weight. She still needed to protect her heart. Hers and Aidan's.

"There's so much to work out." She meant the words to sound strong, yet they were unsure and timid.

"There is." Aidan nuzzled her, scraping her neck with his fangs. "But whether we're destined for each other isn't a question. He's meant to be yours, Rebecca. Just as I am." His moist lips brushed her ear. "He won't touch you unless you give him permission, sweetheart. Do you want him?"

As Aidan spoke to her, she stared at Carson, the need shining in his features combining with the yearning to be with her, with them. She wanted him. More than anything, she wanted him. No, she wanted both men equally. They were *her* men.

"Yes." She whispered the word, her eyes focused intently on Carson's yellowed orbs. "I want him." She reached for the male, the one who'd begun repairing his relationship with Aidan and, by extension, her. She stroked his cheek, running her fingers over his whiskered skin. She traced his lips, feeling the velvety softness beneath her fingertips. "I want you."

"Are you sure?" His words vibrated up her arm, and she hated that this fierce male was hesitant.

"Yes." She retraced her path, ghosting over his cheek and then circling his neck. She gripped him gently and eased him toward her.

Aidan still nuzzled her neck, his cock snug against her pussy, reminding her of his presence. Carson edged forward, and he followed easily, allowing himself to be encouraged until his lips were against hers, his mouth slanting over hers in a passion-inducing kiss.

Carson tasted different than Aidan, sweeter with a razor-edge of heat while his partner was muskier, dark forests. They complemented each other while acting as opposites as well.

His tongue traveled her lips, sliding into her mouth and tasting her, and she did the same, enjoying his flavors. They tangled and stroked, searching and learning while Aidan lurked within reach. Aidan constantly reminded her of his presence as she studied Carson. Lips teasing her, cock exciting her, body surrounding her in a cocoon of pleasure.

Slowly their kiss eased, Carson pulling gently away. "How much of me do you want, Rebecca? I'm yours, what do you want me to give you?"

She knew what he wanted, and she knew she craved the same thing. "Everything, Carson. Everything."

*

The chains holding Carson in place shattered with Rebecca's words, with her plea. The kiss... The kiss had been beautiful, passionate, and gentle in one, teasing him with what could be, while keeping him restrained.

Now, he didn't have to withhold his need. He could unleash his desires for the lush beauty moaning beneath his Alpha partner.

So he did. It took no time and hardly any effort to nudge Aidan aside so he could lick and kiss their mate. Her skin was drugging, tempting and tormenting at the same time. Her breasts were smooth and sleek, her nipples hardened nubs that called for attention.

His cock was rock hard, aching to sink into her, take her and claim her, but that'd require Aidan. Later. He ached to taste her first.

Her stomach was gently rounded, and he imagined her swollen and pregnant with their pups. *Someday...*

The gnarled skin of her lower abdomen met his mouth, the wounds sending a spear of pain into his heart for the agony she must have endured. He laved her right hip, enjoying each gasp and moan that burst from her chest. He had the same sensitive area on his own body now; the location of her Mark would always be a spot that drove them wild.

Then he moved further south, on to lick her pussy, to savor the salty-sweet flavors of her juices and revel in her responses. She was delicious and gorgeous and *theirs*.

So very, very theirs.

His cock throbbed and bobbed inside his boxers, screaming to be released, to sink into her slick warmth. But he refrained. They had a plan. They'd perfected their approach when they shared a woman.

Rebecca isn't just another woman, is she?

She wasn't. So he threw their history out the window and merely focused on Rebecca's pleasure, on her breathy moans and shuddering whines. When the sounds became muted, he raised his gaze from her plump pussy and found Aidan kneeling beside her. Their mate, gaze glazed with passion, sucked his friend's cock, teasing and tempting Aidan with her mouth, sliding over his length before releasing him to gently suckle the head. It wasn't skilled or practiced. No, his mate simply enjoyed exploring his friend, unlike the women in their past. That's what made her different.

She wiggled her hips, taking his attention away from the seductive vision of his partner and mate together, and back to her pink lower lips.

Carson grinned and lapped at her slit, drawing more of her juices over his tongue. "Is this what you want?"

She nodded, and he did it again, enjoying her shudders and moans. He could pleasure her for days, years. Endless years.

But first she had to be claimed, by him, by them.

Carson flicked her clit, rubbing the pleasurable nub in rapid succession before speaking again. "Do you want to belong to us, Rebecca? Are you ready?"

A long, deep groan accompanied her rapid agreement.

That was followed by Aidan's hoarse voice. "God, man, don't ask her questions like that. Nearly came in her mouth, and I don't wanna do that until I'm inside her."

Aidan withdrew, his cock slick with Rebecca's saliva, and a bolt of jealousy struck Carson in the chest. The man had enjoyed their mate's mouth before him.

Then he remembered and reminded himself she was theirs to share forever. They would enjoy her numerous times over the years. Tonight was the first of many.

Aidan remained kneeling beside her head, while Carson remained settled between her thighs. He'd already fucked up once, he wanted her to be crystal fucking clear about what she desired.

"How do you want this? Will Aidan be in your ass? Your pussy? Where do you want me?" He tried to keep his tone level, not giving a hint about what he desired.

Her gaze flicked from him to Aidan and back again, as if asking for permission and confirming they were both on board with what was about to happen.

Fuck yeah, he wanted it, wanted her. More than anything in the world, he desired her.

"I want you…" She blushed, the pink hue belying the sexuality she'd shown moments before. She had no problem sucking cock while he sucked her clit, but saying the words seemed beyond her.

Carson would say them for her. He rose to his knees between her spread thighs. He slid his palms over her skin, making his way to the juncture of her legs. With one finger, he circled her pussy, skimming her soaked warmth. "Do you want me here? Or"—he let his touch travel south until he stroked her hidden rosette—"here?"

Rebecca shook her head.

"So that means this pretty pink pussy is mine," he growled, the wolf pleased they'd have the first chance to impregnate her. The animal was base in its desires. Rebecca. Pups. Caring for Rebecca and their pups.

Rebecca nodded.

Aidan stroked her cheek. "That means I get that lush ass, doesn't it? Carson's gonna lay back, and you're gonna ride him while I prepare you for me." His friend rubbed his thumb over her lip, and she sucked it into her mouth. Damn, he wanted to fuck those pretty lips. "Then I'm going to push my cock into you and you'll scream. You're gonna beg for more and beg us to stop, and when you can't take anymore, we're gonna claim you. My bite's gonna be here." Aidan stroked their mate's left shoulder. "And his will be right here." His partner stroked the right.

It was how they'd discussed it. How they'd imagined claiming their mate. Not necessarily positions, but their desired locations for their claiming bites.

Aidan went left, Carson went right, and then their mate would be locked between them.

Soon...

*

114

It'd be soon. Soon Aidan would push his cock into the tightness of her ass and then she'd be theirs.

Soon. Soon. Soon.

But not soon enough.

While his partner settled in, Aidan bolted and snared his bottle of lube. They'd brought several tubes on the off chance they *did* meet their mate at the Gathering.

By the time he returned, Rebecca was straddling Carson's thighs, rubbing that slick pussy of hers along his length. His friend's hands gripped her hips as he encouraged a gentle rhythm that had her gasping and moaning in equal measure.

"That's so fucking pretty." His mate, lost to the pleasure, was gorgeous.

"Aidan…" Passion glazed her eyes, making her gaze unfocused.

"Take his cock into you, sweetheart. Lemme see you take him." Aidan didn't recognize his own voice, the wolf getting in on the action.

But Rebecca heard him because she rose up, putting space between her and Carson. His friend repositioned his cock and then she was sitting, taking his partner into her body with a soul-deep moan.

"God damn, that's beautiful." He couldn't hold the words in.

"Feels fucking amazing. God, hot and tight." Carson gasped when she rocked her hips.

"What do you think, sweetheart?"

Rebecca leaned back, and he dipped, nuzzling her from behind. "So big. So good."

"It'll feel better when I'm in your ass." Aidan reached around and cupped her breasts, enjoying the weight of her mounds. So large and full and more than filled his palms. He couldn't wait to suckle them again, draw a pebbled nipple into his mouth.

Which meant Carson couldn't either. "Lean down, sweetheart. Let Carson taste your pretty tits."

Rebecca whimpered, and Carson groaned, a look of pain chasing over his features. He imagined their mate clenching around his friend, tightening with her pleasure.

"She likes that idea. A lot."

Aidan chuckled and nudged her. "Give him a taste while I explore this ass."

Another whimper. Another groan.

But she did as he asked, leaning forward, and the two of them became a mass of gentle shifts of body and breathy moans. He should be jealous, but then he stared at her little pucker waiting for his cock and realized: 1) he'd get a chance to fill her pussy later and 2) he really, really wanted to claim her ass.

With slick fingers, he listened to her pleasure-tinged sounds, some accompanying his movements and others with Carson's. It didn't matter who caused her breathy whimpers. His only focus was ensuring none held a hint of pain.

No, when he stretched her ass, preparing her for him, there was nothing but desire coating her.

It felt like hours, his cock throbbing and pulsing, seeming to reach for Rebecca before he determined she was able to take him without pain.

And yet, he still needed to make sure, confirm she wanted to join her life to theirs and tie them together.

"Do you want this, Rebecca?" he murmured, knowing she'd hear him.

She whimpered and nodded, but it wasn't enough.

"I need the words, sweetheart. Do you want to belong to us? It's your last chance to say no. Once the wolf grabs me, he's going to want you." Eyes locked on the curve of her shoulder, he stroked her spine. "It'll crave your blood and he won't be happy until he has it."

"Yes." She turned her head and looked over her shoulder at him. "Make me yours, yours and Carson's."

That was all he needed, all his wolf needed.

Aidan stroked his cock, imagining being inside her. He saw Carson's cock already embedded in her pussy. He'd be there someday, but he always loved a woman's ass. It was tight and warm, but above all, it showed trust. Pure trust that he wouldn't hurt her, that he'd take care of her as he possessed that vulnerable hole.

He rose to his knees, hand gripping the base of his dick as he pointed it toward her entrance. The head of his shaft popped through the outer ring of muscle first, drawing a sharp gasp from his mate. He petted her lower back, easing some of the tension she carried. He fought to remain still, to hold back the desire to enter her in a swift thrust.

"You okay?" He kept his voice low and soothing.

"Fuck yeah, she is. About to strangle my cock. She's squeezing so hard." Carson's words were tight, and Aidan grinned.

Rebecca nodded, her hair sliding over her back.

Taking her action as permission, he eased deeper, groaning and gasping with the tightening sensations. Hot velvet encircled him, pulled him farther into her body. Her ass blossomed and opened for him, accepting him with ease. His mate wanted this, wanted him inside her, and he ached to grant her every wish.

Slowly, so scared of hurting her, he pushed onward, filling her with more and more of his cock until his hips finally came to rest on her ass. He was inside her, possessing and claiming her like no other would again. This body, her pleasure, belonged to him and Carson now.

Forever.

Aidan stroked her back, kneading her muscles, touching as much of her as he could before he returned to her plump ass. They'd had their share of bony women over the years, but they always came back to females with soft curves that would cradle them and, eventually, their pups.

Someday soon... Carson spoke into his mind, the first time since they'd blown up at each other.

Soon... Aidan agreed.

"Are you ready for me to move?" He kept his voice low and soothing. "You need to lay there, let us pleasure you?"

"Do you want that?" Carson echoed him.

Rebecca nodded.

"Not enough, sweetheart." Aidan squeezed her globes tight. "Tell us what you want."

"I want—" Aidan traced her hole where it stretched around his cock, and she gasped, shuddering before she tried again. "I want you to fuck me. I want you to come in me, and I want you to bite me." He loved her little tremble, so he repeated the action. "*Please.*"

"Anything for you, Rebecca." Then, withdrawing slowly and then pushing in with just as much care, Aidan gave her what she desired. "Even if it kills me, I'll give you anything."

*

Anything? No, Rebecca wanted *everything*. All of it. Now and then maybe again later. Okay, again forever and ever.

Especially when Aidan withdrew and then as he re-entered her, it was Carson's turn to retreat. They alternated their thrusts and retreats, always keeping her balanced on the edge.

Large hands gripped her hips, holding her steady as they tormented her. It was too much yet not enough. It was too fucking slow and still too fast. She was out of breath, panting while they took and gave.

Each shift of muscle, each clench and release, gave her more pleasure than the moment before.

She'd never get tired of this, of them.

Slowly the pace and force increased, the hands gripping her hips tightening as they pressed in and out of her. She was lost to the bliss and ecstasy. They didn't use her, and take what they desired. No, they gifted her with just as much joy.

Her nipples were rock hard, stimulated by Carson's mouth and further pleasured as they remained against his chest. Her clit throbbed, pulsing and twitching each time Carson's hips met hers.

She moaned with each meeting of their bodies, gasped when one thrust was more forceful than the last, and whimpered when one of them left her completely. She wanted them inside her, filling her without fail.

"Please," she whimpered. "*Please.*"

She wasn't sure what she asked for, but the word kept rolling through her mind. Please and more and oh, right there.

"We've got you," Aidan grunted. "Right fucking there, sweetheart."

"Fuck, she's tight. Shit, not gonna last."

"Need you." Another whine escaped.

"Gotta come first. Come with us." Aidan snarled, and his words pushed her arousal higher.

Now she knew what they wanted, and she slumped between them, no longer trying to help and merely accepting whatever they wished.

The echoing slap of their bodies meeting was joined by their heaving breaths and quiet begging.

Soon. Soon. Soon.

She knew her release was on the horizon, each movement shoving her toward the precipice and closer to the sky. She wanted to jump off the ledge and see if the men, her mates, would catch her.

She focused on their attentions, on the way Aidan's cock still caused a pleasurable burn and the way Carson's dick stroked her inner walls. Each entrance gifted her with more pleasure. Pleasure that drew her along, teasing her with more bliss and ecstasy.

She followed it, allowed herself to be swept away.

"Gonna…" She was going to come, to scream and cry and revel in their bodies.

"Do it. Come for us." Aidan grunted and then Carson groaned and their sounds of pleasure did it for her.

She was there, jumping off the edge, flying into the air and losing herself to the joy. Her body trembled, a scream building in her throat as it overtook her and then a sharp pain surrounded her shoulders. Growls and snarls accompanied the bites but instead of halting her release, it tripled her body's enjoyment.

She flew higher, dancing through the air, and she recognized the moment her mates joined her, when they succumbed to the pleasure. A new heat filled her, warming her from inside out as those teeth burrowed deeper into her flesh. The pain was nearly overwhelming, but the pleasure that accompanied the wounds overcame any discomfort.

She became a ball of bliss, the sensations encompassing her, and she lost herself. Time held no meaning, not when their mating continued until finally their movements slowed, their lungs no longer billowing air in and out of their bodies. The lessening brought her floating back to reality, and she sighed when she could breathe again.

Fangs slid from her flesh, and two tongues bathed the wounds, her mates taking care of her.

Before long, Aidan slid free of her, drawing a whimper from her throat. Then a whine accompanied Carson's movements when he withdrew from her pussy. She was left bereft, empty of them and unsure of herself.

She needn't have bothered because while they withdrew, it was only to bracket her once again, one mate on each side as hands stroked her. Their voices were soft, kisses gentle while they petted her, praised her. Two tongues laved her wounds, two noses nuzzled her neck, and they each threw a leg over part of her. Aidan's curled around her calf while Carson's molded to her thigh.

Their warmth soothed her, lulled her to sleep. She smiled as she drifted off, a mate on both sides and a smile on her face.

They had issues to sort through, but here, in the bedroom as they shared their bodies, there were none.

CHAPTER ELEVEN

Rebecca woke deliciously sore and bracketed by her mates—
her *mates*. One male on each side, she breathed deeply and
sought out their combined scents. Sure, the musk of sex
hung in the air, and it'd cause some to wrinkle their noses,
but… it was them together and becoming one.

There was nothing stinky about that.

Carson nuzzled her shoulder and squeezed her waist. He'd
done that all night, as if she'd escape and run out on him.
She wiggled against him, reaffirming her presence, and he
immediately settled with a soft sigh.

Aidan was a bit more barbaric. He'd thrown his leg over hers
while wrapping an arm over her chest and cupping her breast
in his large palm. It said she wasn't going anywhere. Period.

Rebecca reveled in the contrasts. In the differences between
her two men.

She still couldn't wrap her mind around that. Two men. One
who'd been damaged by those who supposedly loved him
and another who'd looked past the scars to see a survivor
and one worthy of love. Not that Carson would say the "L"
word toward Aidan, but Rebecca saw it there.

And she was lucky enough to bridge the two. She'd spent her
whole life looking for a man who'd understand her past and
love her not despite it, but because of it. She simply hadn't
realized her perfect man came in a set of two.

Rebecca shifted in their hold, enjoying the tightening of arms and the low growl from Aidan followed by the gentle whine from Carson. Such sweet men even though they'd rip out the throat of anyone who threatened her.

Threat... The word reminded her of her sisters. She wasn't sure if Lorelei and Paisley had been hauled to the Gathering, and part of her hoped they'd been spared the ordeal. *She* was thrilled with the outcome, but she wasn't a fan of the danger that accompanied these two men.

Her body reminded her it was morning and it had its own round of "needs" that didn't involve men and their mouths, fingers, or cocks.

She wiggled, testing their unconscious resolve to keep her in place, and found they were really, really determined for her to stay put.

Great.

She tried again, scooching down instead of trying to sit up. That got her free of Carson's gentle embrace but still left her with Aidan's proprietary hold.

There was nothing for it. Damn it.

Rebecca prodded the arm still wrapped around her chest. When that didn't get a response, she poked harder, determined to wake the man. He'd fucked her into a stupor last night and made her scream so loud she was sure the entire hotel heard. The least he could do was let her up so she could pee.

Another jab and still he didn't move.

What wonderful protectors they turned out to be. They couldn't even bother to—

A loud yell came from the living area, the voice familiar even if she didn't know the woman too well. The first was followed by two others, and she realized Scarlet, Gabby, and Whitney had somehow gotten into their suite.

And while Rebecca's nudges didn't get her men moving, those invaders did.

Aidan and Carson leapt from the bed in a flurry of sheets and fur. She'd seen a handful of wolves shift by now, but she'd never witnessed the speed her mates exhibited. By the time the first blanket was tossed aside, they were shifted. Hell, human feet never even touched the carpet. It was all paws.

They raced around the bed, placing their bodies between her and the door. Their muscles were bunched and tight, wolves ready to pounce and destroy whoever walked into their space.

The handles on the doors turned, disengaging the latch, and then the panel swung open. The moment it separated from the frame, the growls began, both Aidan and Carson voicing their displeasure while also threatening the interlopers.

Scarlet stepped in and didn't seem to give a damn Rebecca's mates were pretty intent on tearing her to shreds.

"Um, guys?" Maybe they couldn't think and understand when wolfy. Sure, Scarlet told her they were completely cognizant, but she was starting to doubt that assertion.

Scarlet eased further into the room, ignoring the snarling wolves and smiling at Rebecca instead. "Hey, how are ya?"

"Aidan? Carson?" Worry filled her tone, and she hoped they sensed her panic and would cut the crap out already.

"Oh, don't worry about them." Scarlet pulled her hand from behind her back, and Rebecca hadn't realized she'd been hiding anything. Then she groaned at what the woman revealed. She shook it, jingling ball filling the air with the tinkling of metal on metal. "What's this?" She adopted the excited tone a person would use with a… puppy. Rebecca moaned. "That's right. Who's got the ball? Want the ball? Do you want the ball?" Scarlet shook it again and then turned and tossed it into the living area. "There goes the ball. Get it now. Get it!"

Her mates' growls didn't cease. If anything, they grew in volume.

Those growls were joined by a handful of others, and then more people filled the entryway. Sure, Gabby and Whitney sauntered in, but they were followed by their mates. God, the whole family arrived.

Rebecca hauled the blanket higher to cover more of her skin. The important pink bits were hidden, but she didn't want *anyone* looking at *any* part of her.

"Scarlet," Madden growled at his mate and thankfully didn't look in Rebecca's direction.

"What?" The woman adopted an innocent expression that didn't seem to fool anyone. "I thought I'd give them a little morning exercise. I mean, I'm sure that when we have pups they'll enjoy chasing the ball. Won't they? What's the fun in having a puppy if you can't—"

Keller's hand covered Scarlet's mouth, silencing her. "When we have pups, you will not have them play fetch." Hand still in place, Keller turned his attention to Rebecca, Aidan, and Carson. "We apologize for intruding—"

Gabby raised her hand. "I'm not apologizing."

That earned Gabby a glare from Jack and a grin from Berke.

"Look, we only came to see what Rebecca thought of being mated and to make sure she was okay." Whitney smiled wide.

Rebecca furrowed her brow. "How did you know I'd mate them?"

"Uh, hello, I may be mated but—" Whitney's gaze enveloped Aidan and Carson. "When they're on two legs… *damn.*"

Suddenly Whitney's mouth was covered by Emmett *and* Levy's hands.

It looked like Jack and Berke had the same idea with Gabby, but she ducked before they made contact.

"Wait! I have one question, and it's sort of a family tradition thing and then we can be all serious." When Jack and Berke remained frozen, Rebecca's cousin stood. "Now, we wanted to know what you thought of mating sex."

"Umm…" Her mates looked back at her, the same question in their gazes. "It was awesome?" Okay, it sounded more like a question than a statement. She tried again. "Yeah, awesome."

Unfortunately, Gabby did not look thrilled with Rebecca's answer. The woman wailed and pouted. "No, the answer is squishy. Scarlet said squishy, and I said squishy and Whitney said squishy and it's a family tradition so say the fucking word already." Gabby looked pretty damned scary. "Now." Gabby straightened her shirt. "Rebecca, what do you think of mating sex?"

Gabby repeated the question so slowly that Rebecca knew there was only one answer she could give if she wanted to continue living.

"Squishy."

"*Awesome.*" Gabby waved at Keller and Madden, then Jack and Berke. "We're done now, you can uncover their mouths. We gotta talk about Lorelei and Paisley."

Rebecca's heart thundered, picking up an unnatural pace. "What about them?"

Before anyone could answer, she was swept into Aidan and Carson's embrace. The men shifted so fast, racing to her side before she could blink. Their thick, muscular arms embraced her while their presence comforted her more than anything in the world. Their hold told her she could fall, and they'd be there to catch her.

Scarlet eased closer and sat on the bench at the end of the bed. Concern was etched into her features. Concern and sadness. "They're here at the Gathering."

Rebecca swallowed hard and settled her head against Carson's shoulder while blindly reaching for Aidan. He was there, her powerful rock. They were at the Gathering, which meant they were either Alpha Marked and Rebecca had never known, or they were Warden Born which had been hidden from the anti-wolf part of her family. Regardless, their presence also meant their lives depended on enveloping them in the safety of their family.

Theirs. The Wickhams and Twynhams tied together again.

"Did—" She coughed and cleared her throat, trying to banish the lump that'd formed. "Did Miles and Holden find them? Where are they?"

Scarlet frowned and grimaced. "The thing about it is…"

Nothing good was ever revealed in a sentence that began in that way. Nothing.

So, with her mates at her side, warm fingers brushing her, hands supporting her, she found out Lorelei and Paisley were nowhere to be found. At least, not yet.

Rebecca hoped they'd be discovered soon because she couldn't look toward her future with Aidan and Carson without ensuring her sisters would find the same happiness.

Tears stung her eyes, worry over the werewolves from the five families finding her sisters before they could hitting her hard. What if they were captured? Tortured? Beaten and killed? What if…

A sob tore from her throat.

"Shh…" Carson hugged her tight while Aidan ran his fingers through her hair.

"We'll find them, sweetheart, and I'll tear apart anyone who's even looked at them funny." If it weren't for the pure rage filling Aidan's gentle tone, she would have laughed.

"And I'll help him chop them into tiny pieces." Carson added his own macabre promise.

She turned her attention to Carson, tilting her head back until she could meet his gaze. She released the first words that came to mind, the first ones that burst from her heart and rose to her lips. They didn't care that she'd just met them, that it was fast or too soon or any other idea that told her it couldn't be real. Because these feelings, these emotions, didn't get any more real than what they'd shared and what they would share for the rest of their lives.

"I love you."

Rebecca ignored the shininess of his eyes and merely listened to the words when Carson replied. "I love you, too."

The hand stroking her head fisted her strands and forced Rebecca to turn her attention to Aidan.

"And me? I'm doing the heavy lifting; he's acting as the chef. Anyone can chop things into tiny pieces. They can't all gut a man with one swipe," he grumbled.

Rebecca grinned and reached for her gruff mate, pulling him close until he almost lay atop her. Carson took more of her weight as Aidan covered her. She stroked his cheek, tracing the lines of his face and looking past the scars. "I love you."

Aidan grunted. "Good."

Scarlet cut in. "You're supposed to say it back." All three of them glared at the Ruling Alpha Mate. "What? Just sayin'."

Aidan nuzzled her cheek and placed his warm, moist lips against the shell of her ear. "Love you, too."

Rebecca's heart filled with emotion, with love, and hope. The worry for her sisters still lingered, still filled her with dread, but she knew with her mates at her side, they'd find Lorelei and Paisley.

Then Aidan and Carson would kill anyone who'd hurt them.

They'd be all bloody, but that's why God created showers.

THE END

If you enjoyed Rebecca, please be totally awesomesauce and leave a review so others may discover it as well. Long review or short, your opinion will help other readers make future purchasing decisions. So, go forth and rate my level-o-awesome!

By the way… you can check at the rest of the Alpha Marked series on Celia's website: http://celiakyle.com/alphamarked

ABOUT CELIA KYLE

Ex-dance teacher, former accountant and erstwhile collectible doll salesperson, New York Times and USA Today bestselling author Celia Kyle now writes paranormal romances for readers who:

1) Like super hunky heroes (they generally get furry)
2) Dig beautiful women (who have a few more curves than the average lady)
3) Love laughing in (and out of) bed.

It goes without saying that there's always a happily-ever-after for her characters, even if there are a few road bumps along the way.

Today she lives in Central Florida and writes full-time with the support of her loving husband and two finicky cats.

If you'd like to be notified of new releases, special sales, and get FREE eBooks, subscribe here:
http://celiakyle.com/news

You can find Celia online at:
http://celiakyle.com
http://facebook.com/authorceliakyle
http://twitter.com/celiakyle

COPYRIGHT PAGE